Charlie Mcgee
and the Leprechaun

Charlie McGee and the Leprechaun

Life's Curious Twist of Events

R. C. JETTE

RESOURCE *Publications* • Eugene, Oregon

CHARLIE MCGEE AND THE LEPRECHAUN
Life's Curious Twist of Events

Resource Publications
An Imprint of Wipf and Stock Publishers
199 W. 8th Ave., Suite 3
Eugene, OR 97401

www.wipfandstock.com

PAPERBACK ISBN: 978-1-5326-7828-8
HARDCOVER ISBN: 978-1-5326-7829-5
EBOOK ISBN: 978-1-5326-7830-1

Manufactured in the U.S.A.   FEBRUARY 7, 2019

This book is dedicated to the Lord that gives life and to my husband who has always encouraged me to go forward and believe that I can do it no matter how flooded the Jordan may seem.

A special thanks to Wipf and Stock Publishers for making it all possible, for their professional staff who worked so patiently with me, and for accepting what others rejected by publishing: *Storms Are Faith's Workout: Preparing Christians for Spiritual Ambush* (non-fiction, September 27, 2018); *The Elfdins and the Gold Temple: An Oralee Chronicle* (fiction, October 10, 2018).

And we know that all things work together for good to them that love God, to them who are the called according to his purpose

ROMANS 8:28 KJV

Contents

Prologue

TEAGUE WAS NOT YOUR ordinary Leprechaun by any means. He was not at all content with making shoes or mending them for that matter. It seems that this young Leprechaun of one hundred years was quite taken with shenanigans. His playful activities were focused on the "trooping fairies" who became rather annoyed by his tomfoolery.

Teague would hide their green jackets and place red ones like his in their place, or he would hide their food, dishes, and even some of their furniture. His whole undertaking was spent on practical jokes that left the fairies in continuous mayhem to find this or to find that. They were beside themselves with his constant interfering with their daily life. It seemed their whole colony was in regular chaos because of this Leprechaun and his pranks.

Although the fairies figured that Teague had a good deal to learn, they decided that enough was enough. A secret vote was taken while the Leprechaun was away with his treasure. Through a unanimous vote, they decided that it was time to rid themselves of this Leprechaun's trickery. They watched and waited until after he had settled down for the night and then sprinkled fairy dust on him. As soon as the dust fell on him, he plunged into a deep sleep.

While he was in that intense slumber, they tied him up with magical fairy rope, carried him to the Irish Sea, and dropped him in. Of course, everyone that knows anything about Leprechauns is aware that they can't swim. This was in fact meant to be the end of Teague and not just his trickery. However, when he hit the water, he suddenly woke up, recognized his dilemma, and began to scream for help.

> *"Someone help me please;*
> *This is no tease.*
> *It seems I'm a victim;*
> *Fer I cannot swim.*
> *This rope is fairy magic;*
> *And fer me quite tragic."*

He was so involved in his trouble that he forgot that he was not invisible. Nevertheless, this became the means in which his deliverance was made possible.

Apparently, a human named Charlie thought he was seeing and hearing things as he walked along the shore. For everyone comprehends knowing about the existence of Leprechauns and seeing them are two different things. But, the more Teague shrieked repeatedly, Charlie realized that he was hearing one of the little people call for help. With that revelation, he jumped into the water, quickly swam to the little man, and pulled him to shore.

But when Teague looked at him, Charlie jumped back in fear. Teague knew that he couldn't untie himself from the magic rope of the fairies, so he spoke.

> *"Don't ye be a fool;*
> *I didn't jump into the pool.*
> *If ye cut me loose,*
> *Me power, I will not use."*

Charlie cut him loose, and Teague just sat quietly for what seemed forever to Charlie. Then slowly the Leprechaun stood up and declared.

> *"I vow to end,*
> *And surely mend,*
> *Me life of joking,*
> *And others wounding."*

The fairies had finally gotten through to Teague who now realized that life is not meant to have fun at someone else's expense.

By this time, he appreciated that he had been rescued by a human.

> *"I thank ye me lad;*
>> *You've made me quite glad.*
> *Me life ye did save;*
>> *Who was such a knave.*
> *I do swear to change;*
>> *And me life to rearrange.*
> *Ye shall be me friend;*
>> *And me ways I'll surely mend."*

Determined to rectify his ways, he chose to befriend this human that had saved his life. Charlie became confidant to Teague's deepest secrets and was permitted to see all his treasures, which included his favorite magical green amulet.

I

The Peculiar Birthday Card

CHARLIE MCGEE HAD TAKEN on the responsibility of being the man about the farm for his widowed Mum since his Pa's death. A vigorous worker who did a man's job since he was eleven, Charlie was respected by all of Hart County. His best friend, besides Colin Coyle, was his dog Toby, a black and silver German shepherd, who was his constant companion. Together they'd do the chores and go on adventures throughout the hundred acres as if exploring new lands.

This day was an extra special day, for it was Charlie's sixteenth birthday. He found himself giggling all day and it was difficult to keep his mind on his duties. With his hands on his hips, he sighed heavily and perused the barn to make sure he finished everything. The plow horses were in their stalls with fresh hay in their trough, the milking cows were back in the field, chickens, ducks, geese, goats, rabbits, et cetera were fed. All the stalls and the floor had been mucked out and fresh hay scattered on the floor. The bridles and leads were hanging on their hooks; the blankets were hanging on the front of the stalls. "Good." He exhaled. "I can't let my excitement interfere with my properly completing all that has to be done before lunch." His eyes caught sight of a plate of apple and carrot slices on an empty barrel. "Oh no!" He said grabbing his head with both hands. "I forgot all about feeding Casey."

He hurried up, grabbed the carrot and apple slices, and ran over to feed his horse. Feeling his stomach knot up, he fed the treat to his horse with his right hand and rubbed the horse's neck with his left hand. "I am so sorry, Casey." He stomped the floor with his right foot. "Birthday or not, I have to keep my mind on responsibility. My Pa would not have forgotten to feed his horse, no matter the day." After Casey enjoyed his special treat, Charlie filled his hay trough with fresh hay and then he filled the water trough with fresh water from the well.

When he had finished, he placed his hands on his hips and with a sigh of relief, his eyes once again examined the barn. "Yes, everything is complete for now." He gave a nod and headed for the tall double doors. "Let's go Toby." He turned to look at his dog and chuckled. "You don't want me to close the doors with you inside, do you?" Toby ran around him and was out the door ahead of Charlie and practically ran into the chickens wandering the yard and pecking at bugs in the dirt. The dog quickly gained his composure and turned around and gave a bark. "Okay, I'm hurrying," Charlie laughed as he closed the doors.

Life was difficult at times for Charlie without his Pa. He dearly missed the man who was an incredible influence in his life. His Pa was a hard worker who taught Charlie the necessity of being responsible and taking on one's duty with a willing heart. He could still hear his Pa's words in his mind. "Always remember that taking care of others is a privilege and honor. Do your responsibility with a willing heart and you will find pleasure in what you do."

Charlie understood those words of wisdom, for he took pleasure in helping his widowed Mum. The thought of her brought a smile to his face. All morning, she'd pretended to forget that today was his birthday. But Charlie had smelled the chocolate cake baking while doing his chores. And yesterday, he'd gotten a quick look of a neatly wrapped package before his Mum dashed into her room. He was sure that she had made him a new Sunday suit for church. When they were at the local merchant's last month, he observed her looking at the material and whisper to Mr. O'Malley, the owner.

His stomach growled as he hurried to the house with Toby close at his heels. It's a long time from breakfast till lunch for a young lad. When he opened the kitchen door, his Mum greeted him with a big hug. "Happy Birthday, luv." Maggie McGee grinned and ruffled her son's red ringlets. "I couldn't go another moment with you thinking that I forgot your birthday." She pointed towards the dry sink holding a ceramic bowl and pitcher. "Get yourself washed for lunch. We'll celebrate your birthday tonight at supper when Dr. Dixon and Chelsea arrive. You know they wouldn't miss this for anything. After all, you are their godson." She sighed. "They love you like you were their own lad."

She turned to go toward the cast iron wood burning stove, stopped and turned back again. "Oh yes, Colin sent a note saying that Mr. O'Hara can't spare him today. They have an overload of shoes to get done. He felt terrible about missing your birthday but said that he'll see you Sunday at church and for his usual Sunday lunch with us." She threw her hands up in the air. "Where's my blooming mind? Father Flanagan is waiting in the parlor. He said that you told him that he could come and get that calf at his convenience. It seems that he has the butcher lined up first thing tomorrow morning."

Charlie gestured with his hands. "Well, I'll have to postpone my wash for a bit." He hurried toward the parlor where Father Flanagan was waiting. As he entered the parlor, he found Father Flanagan seated in one of the Queen Anne chairs with cabriole legs. The priest was so engrossed in reading the family Bible that he almost dropped it as Charlie entered the room. He let out a heavy sigh and quickly blessed himself. "I thought that while I was waiting, I would use the time wisely and read my scripture text for Sunday's Mass." He placed the Bible down on the oval top trestle table with a key-tenoned center rail and turned spindle supports. When he stood up, he reached into his pocket and pulled out a pouch of money. "Here's the price that you asked for the calf. I hope this hasn't proven to be an inconvenient time for you." He bit the hangnail on his left thumb. "It seems that I forgot today was your birthday, until your Mum reminded me. However, I will at this time give you a birthday blessing." He reached into his other pocket and pulled out a vial of oil and proceeded to give Charlie the blessing. "In the Name of the Father, the Son, and the Holy Ghost, I ask you Blessed Savior to bless this birthday as no other."

"Thank you, Father," Charlie said as he shook the priest's hand, "a blessing is always welcomed." He gestured with his hands. "Well, I guess that we had better go get that calf. He's a hefty one, that's for sure. I believe that he's put on about ten more pounds since you saw him. The butcher won't have any problem getting plenty of meat from him."

After Charlie had taken care of Father Flanagan, he hurried into the kitchen. "Sorry, Mum, I hope everything didn't get too cold. But I didn't want to seem like I was rushing Father Flanagan. He's a busy man, and I know that he has to do what he can when he can." He chuckled. "Besides, I really like him. I look forward to hearing his sermons about Bible stories. He makes everything so interesting."

Mrs. McGee smiled. "I kept it all on the stove to keep warm. Everything is fine. Besides, your responsibility had to be carried out. I had asked Father Flanagan to stay for lunch, but he had some appointments this afternoon." She wiped her face with her apron. "That priest has been a godsend since he arrived from Ireland about thirty years ago. This was his first parish as a young priest. The old folks say that he's not like the priests that were here before; he's always looking for ways to help the people. I do believe that he truly goes the extra mile when it comes to helping. Never has he seen anyone in need and not done all that he can to help. He's what I call a real saint." She started to set the scrolled trestle table of key-tenon design and turned to look at Charlie. "Don't forget that your godparents will be here for supper. So, you will have extra pressure to get the feeding and other chores done because of the time lost this afternoon. I know that it will not be the same without Colin, but that boy has a heavy load on his shoulders also." She motioned to the dry sink. "I think you can finally wash for lunch."

She chuckled. "We will have to eat a little faster than normal, but I think that my hunger will require a little speed."

Charlie nodded and headed to the dry sink holding the bowl to wash. He poured water from the pitcher into the bowl and began to wash his hands. He'd be glad to see Dr. Dixon and Chelsea, but he will miss Colin. Charlie's Pa and the doctor had been friends most of their life. In honor of that friendship, Rory McGee named his son Charles Dixon McGee. Colin Coyle, on the other hand was Charlie's best friend. Although Colin was seventeen, they'd been like brothers ever since Charlie could remember. Colin with his straight black hair and hazel eyes contrasted with Charlie's curly red hair and sky-blue eyes. Although they looked like opposites, they were alike in being hard workers doing all that they could to help their widowed Mums.

Whenever Charlie thought that he had a lot of responsibility with the farm, Colin would come to his mind. Colin was the eldest of six children. He had four sisters ages fifteen, thirteen, eleven, nine and a younger brother age seven who was only a year old when Colin's Pa died. With so many mouths to feed, Colin worked at Olney Junction in Kade County, the next county over, for Shawn O'Hara, the shoemaker. The ironic thing to Charlie is that they both lost their Pa's at eleven years of age.

Charlie's thoughts were interrupted by his Mum's voice. "Are you going to wash all day? I have your place set."

Charlie grinned as he sauntered over to the table and sat down at the opposite end of the table on his Governor Carver arm chair. "I knew you didn't forget my birthday. Did you really think that you could bake a cake and I wouldn't get a whiff of it?"

Maggie giggled. "I should have known. Your Pa was the same. I couldn't put anything past his nose." She took on a haunted look. "He would be so proud of you. I sorely miss him." She straightened up. "He would not want me being melancholy when we are supposed to be celebrating your birthday."

Charlie tilted his head. "I think I heard a horse ride up. We're not expecting anyone are we?"

Maggie was about to pour their milk, paused, and put the pitcher down. "I believe it may be Marvin with mail, but he's late today." She shrugged her shoulders with a sigh. When she went outside, she greeted the carrier who was sitting on his horse with a satchel hanging on each side. "Hello, Marvin, you're late today. Is everything okay?"

"I'm fine, Mrs. McGee, outside of a little gout acting up. Can't complain though, I'm doing just fine." He reached into the satchel on his right and pulled out an envelope. "Here's one for Charlie. It must be a card or something."

Maggie smiled. "Yes, today is Charlie's sixteenth birthday."

"Well, you be sure and wish that lad a happy birthday from me." He closed the satchel. "That lad of yours is one to be mighty proud of. The way he's taken over this farm at such a young age is something to be admired."

"I couldn't be prouder of him. He is a hard worker just like his Pa was." She nodded her head. "Charlie will be pleased by your wishing him a happy birthday." She paused. "You have a blessed day and tell your wife that I'll show her how to make those aprons as soon as she gets the material."

"I sure will, and you have a blessed day. I'll see you and Charlie at Mass on Sunday."

Maggie walked back into the house and handed the envelope to Charlie. "Marvin said to wish you a happy birthday." She gestured towards the card. "It must be a birthday card from someone trying to surprise you, for I saw no return address on it." She turned and started to fill their cups with milk.

Charlie opened the envelope and read the card inside and screwed up his face in puzzlement.

> *"Charlie, did ye think ye got away?*
> *Why did Teague ye disobey?*
> *Did ye forget the power of old?*
> *Say not, ye were not told.*
> *Ye alone chose this fate,*
> *When friendship ye did abdicate.*

As brother to brother we were,
Till toward evil, ye did stir.
Ye took a charm to the green,
And hid in the night unseen,
Ye stole what was mine,
Now green, ye shall shine."

Charlie's eyebrows squeezed together. "Mum! Look at the saying in this card. Talk about being daft. It's a poem that sounds like someone is angry because his friend stole something. It's rather a baffle."

Maggie McGee turned to face her lad. At the sight of him, her body stiffened, and her eyes widened.

Charlie gasped at the sight of his Mum and dropped the card in his lap. "What's wrong? Are you in pain? What is it?"

Maggie slapped her chest and cleared her throat. "Either I'm losing me blooming mind, or I'm really seeing green." She grabbed the table, slowly sat in her chair, and rubbed her eyes. "Hurry! Go to the looking glass. This is all too much."

"What do you mean look in the looking glass? Whatever for? What's real?"

"I believe the looking glass will tell you what is real."

"Mum, what are you talking about? You're scaring me. You're not acting normal." He picked up the card from his lap. "Why the looking glass? Oh blessed St. Patrick!" He exclaimed, as he noticed that his hands were a glowing green. He immediately stood up and ran to the looking glass, which image reflected that he was a bright glowing green. The only thing not green was his red hair. "I look like a blooming Christmas tree all lit up with a red top."

Toby came into the room and barked incessantly. Charlie cried, "Toby, it's me. Don't be afraid." Toby was frenzied at the sight of Charlie. The dog ran around in circles and barked incessantly.

Mrs. McGee tried to quiet the dog to no avail. "I can't think with all this barking. I'll just have to put him in the spare bedroom."

When she returned, Charlie was pacing up and down the room. He all but screamed. "Blessed St. Patrick! What's it all about? Is this supposed to be a birthday joke? There must be an answer."

He stopped and looked at his Mum. "Father Flanagan gave me a blessing. He asked the Lord to bless this birthday as no other." He threw up his hands. "Surely this can't be considered a blessing as no other?"

"I'm sure this has nothing to do with the priest's blessing." She shook her head. "There has to be an explanation." She motioned with her hands for him to be calm. "You have to calm down and let me think. I need to see if I can understand what's going on." She stared at him while her left hand fingered the silver cross on a silver chain around her neck. "It looks like green slime or something all lit up. The glow is frightening. No wonder Toby was so afraid." She crossed her arms and observed her lad. "I wonder if it can be washed off."

"Yes. Yes. Of course," Charlie said, nodding his head. "Why didn't I think of that? That's the solution. I'll just take a bath. That'll do it. I'm sure."

Charlie took hot water from the stove, poured it into the washtub, grabbed clean clothes, closed the door, undressed, sat in the tub, soaped the rag, scrubbed hard, but the green brightened. The more he scrubbed, the more it glowed. He dried himself, put on his clothes, and opened the door. His Mum looked, but Charlie uttered her thought. "It's brighter. It's like luminous. The more that I scrubbed, the brighter it became. It seems to glow more brilliant the longer that I'm green." He held his head with both hands. "Mum, what can I do?"

Maggie shook her head. "I've never heard of a glowing green slime disease." She fingered her silver cross with her left hand. "Have you been near any strange plants? Was there anything unusual in the fields? Did you eat something different?"

Charlie threw up his hands. "No. I know every tree and plant on our land. I've not seen anything unusual; everything's the same as always. You know that Pa taught me not to eat anything that I didn't know." He grabbed his head with both hands and looked around. "Mum, please help me." He ran to the window and closed the draperies. "Don't let anyone see me like this. Tell them I left town or something." He threw up his hands. "How am I going to hide myself? This green is lighting up the whole room. It's like a hundred or more candles glowing. We won't need any lamps or candles burning tonight."

Maggie motioned with her hands for him to calm down. "Please, you must calm down. We have to think."

Charlie didn't seem to hear what his mother said and continued to pace up and down with hands flying. "I'm not going out like this. What if I'm seen? I'll scare Upton Town half to death. They'll lock me away. I'll be put into quarantine." He paused momentarily, let out a heavy sigh, and continued with his pacing. "They'll send me to a circus. I look like a blooming freak show. Who ever heard of a person turning into a green glow? It's like I'm not even human. They'll think that I'm an alien, if there were any such a thing as aliens." He stopped his ranting and with his right hand, he pointed to the spare room door. "Even Toby won't come near me. That tells us how frightening I am." He started pacing again. "Maybe I caught some kind of a rare jungle disease that can't be cured." He threw up his arms. "But there isn't even any jungle near here. How did I catch a rare jungle disease? I've never even been to the jungle. Besides, I don't even know where the nearest jungle is."

Maggie motioned with her hands for him to calm down. "Charlie, you have to calm down. I'm just as befuddled as you. But we've got to keep our heads." She gave out a heavy sigh. "Your Pa would have handled this calmly. We need to remember his example. The situation won't be helped by getting flustered. Remember your Pa always taught that things can't be seen in the right perspective when emotions are in turmoil." She fingered her silver cross with her left hand. "I know that Dr. Dixon and Chelsea will be here this evening at six, but that's almost five hours away. My only concern in waiting is that it may be something really dangerous and contagious." She looked at her hands. "It can't be contagious, or I would be green by now." She paused and looked at her lad. "Are you feeling any pain? Do you feel sick?" She walked over to him and placed her right hand on his forehead. "Well, you're not running a fever. You're as cool as a cucumber." She placed her hands on her hips and bit her bottom lip. "Do you want me to fetch the doctor now, or should we just wait until they get here tonight?"

Charlie took a deep breath and gave a heavy sigh. "You're right. I can't go on like this or I might make myself sick. In fact, I really feel fine." He gestured with his hands. "If I didn't see this green, I wouldn't think that anything was wrong with me. This has me befuddled. I'm in a straight." He pulled out his chair and sat down at the table. "Maybe we should just eat our meal and wait for my godparents to come. After all, I still have to finish my day's work before they come. Pa wouldn't let any glowing green slime disease stop him from his obligations. I must remain level headed and wait for the doctor. Besides, I really have to finish plowing the south field this afternoon."

Maggie gave her lad a loving smile. "Yes, dear, you are so much like your Pa. He would have said the same thing. It seems that his Pa taught him to be responsible just as your Pa taught you."

2

Birthdays Should Be Celebrated

DR. CHARLES DIXON AND his wife, Chelsea, finished up their work as soon as possible. They wouldn't miss Charlie's birthday celebration for anything, not if they could help it. That lad was the closest thing to a son that they had. Although they had wanted children, they remained childless. In the end, after Rory's death, they both felt that it was because of Charlie that they had no lad of their own. Charlie would need all the support that they could give him.

Charles had met Chelsea while they were in college. He was studying to be a doctor, and she was studying to be a nurse. Because her degree took less time than his, she graduated before him. The day after her graduation, they were married with Rory and Maggie McGee as witnesses.

Chelsea worked as a nurse at the nearby hospital, so they could rent an apartment while he finished his doctoral degree. Once he graduated, they moved to his home town of Upton in Hart County to set up practice in his childhood home. Inheriting the home and with Chelsea as Charles's nurse, it made things quite easy for them to get started. Neither of them had any siblings or living parents. Chelsea's parents died of an influenza epidemic when she started her last year of college, and Charles's parents died in an accident just before he graduated.

Charles clutched his bag and Chelsea grabbed Charlie's birthday gift. "Well," Charles said as they headed toward the door, "I'm sure looking forward to this night." He gave a chuckle. "I noticed that Charlie's leather hat is quite worn out and doesn't seem to fit him right anymore."

Chelsea straightened the bow on the package with her right hand. "I believe that he will be quite pleased. He is such a good lad." She closed the door behind them. "I wish some of the other lads in this town were more like him, especially that Peter Smith. That boy is a disgrace; all he does is look for ways to annoy people." Charles gave her a hand up into the buggy, and then he went around and took his place in the buggy next to her. "Of course," Chelsea continued, "Colin Coyle is another good boy taking on the responsibility for that large family." She paused rubbing her left forefinger behind her left ear. "But our godson just brings tears to my eyes at such devotion in helping his widowed mother. After all, she doesn't have four girls to help around the house like Mrs. Coyle."

Charles Dixon took the reins. "Walk on, Daisy." He sat back and made himself comfortable. "I know what you mean about Charlie's devotion. He is the image of his Pa not only in that he's Rory's double, tall and strong-featured, with sky-blue eyes, and a head full red ringlets. But he has the same determination to fulfill his responsibility without complaints." He paused and let out a deep sigh. "It's still so difficult for me to talk about Rory, even after five years. We were more like brothers than friends." He gave a laugh and went back against his seat. "I know you've heard this story a thousand times from Rory and me. But it still amuses me every time I remember the first occasion that Rory and I told someone that we were twins. The person didn't believe us and asked our birth date. When we told him that we were both born on July 10, he scratched his head and told us that we didn't even look alike."

As they travelled out to visit Charlie, Chelsea looked at her husband with such pride. He was a striking man of five foot eight inches, medium build and white hair. She was still amazed at how his hair turned white. When they received the news that Rory had an accident and was found dead, Charles went into temporary shock. The next morning, he walked into the kitchen for breakfast and his hair was completely white at the age of thirty-seven.

Charles sat back in the buggy and enjoyed the scenery and found himself reminiscing about the old days with Rory. Outside of the Wilson spread of two hundred acres, Rory's parents had inherited the next best acreage in Hart County. It had an excellent fishing pond that he and Rory fished regularly. There was also a pond with a spring in the center that kept fresh water bubbling up continuously. He and Rory used to love to swim in that cool water on hot Sunday afternoons. He never thought that he'd be heading to Rory's house and there would be no Rory. Some things are just too hard to understand, but he would honor Rory's memory by being the best godfather possible to Charlie. His thoughts were interrupted by his wife's question. "Do you think that we could travel to Olney Junction? Shawn O'Hara sent a note that my shoes were ready."

"W-what did you say?"

"I questioned if we could go to Olney Junction to pick up my shoes. Shawn O'Hara sent a note to say they were ready."

"Sorry, but my mind was off." He turned to face his wife. "Of course, we'll take a ride out there after Sunday Mass."

She patted her husband's leg. "I'll pack us a picnic lunch and we'll just make it a nice leisurely day of rest."

By this time, they had arrived at Charlie's. Both were taken aback by the green glow coming from the window in the door at the back porch. Chelsea was the first to speak. "That's a strange light for a candle. I don't believe that I've seen that color before. It sure is bright."

Dr. Dixon got down from the buggy, tied the reins around the column of the porch, and helped his wife step down. "It sure does glow. Talk about a strange . . ."

Before he could finish, Maggie came running out to them. Her pallid face gave them both a start. "Please, hurry in. I don't want Charlie to get concerned, but I'm all astonishment at this thing."

Dr. Dixon grabbed her arm. "What's wrong? Is Charlie hurt?" By this time, his hands started to tremble. "Please tell me what's wrong."

Maggie took a deep breath and let out a heavy sigh. "We don't know what it is. That's why we've been waiting for you both to arrive. It's beyond our knowledge."

Chelsea grabbed the doctor's bag and the present. "Let's just get inside."

Maggie hurried to the door with Charles and Chelsea close at her heels. As she opened the door to the kitchen, the green glow became brighter and brighter. When they stepped into kitchen, they were both momentarily disarmed. Charlie looked like glowing green slime. Their years in the medical field enabled them both to keep their composure.

Dr. Dixon addressed Charlie. "When did this happen?"

"This afternoon," Maggie replied.

Before the doctor could say anything else to Charlie, he had run to his room. He immediately returned with the card in his hand and handed it to Dr. Dixon. "It all began after I read that card."

Dr. Dixon read the strange poetic message and screwed up his face. Before he said anything, he handed it to Chelsea. She read it and shook her head in disbelief. The doctor returned his attention toward Charlie. "Who sent it? Where did it come from?"

Charlie shrugged his shoulders. "We have no idea. Mum thought it was a birthday card and gave it to me after Marvin delivered it just before we had lunch."

Dr. Dixon rubbed his forehead with his right hand. "Was there anything else in the envelope like a plant or an insect?"

Charlie shook his head. "Not a thing. It was just the card. I'm just scared that it may be catchy." He gestured towards his Mum. "But Mum doesn't think it's contagious, because she hasn't turned green."

By this time, Chelsea was checking to see if he had a fever. "He's not hot." She gestured with her hands. "He seems fine."

"That was one of the first things that I did," Maggie said as she turned her attention to Dr. Dixon. "Do you have any idea what it is? Can you help us? Do you think that he caught it from the card?"

"I'll do what I can." He opened his bag to take out his stethoscope. "I don't see how a card could have anything to do with this." He turned to his wife. "Do you see any link to this from that card?"

She shook her head. "I've never heard of anyone catching something from a card with a ridiculous poem on it. I mean, really, Charles that does seem to be a bit farfetched."

He chuckled. "I quite agree, but I always like a second opinion."

Chelsea looked at Maggie. "You're both sure that nothing else was in the envelope?"

Maggie shrugged her shoulders. "I didn't see Charlie open it" She gestured with her left hand towards the table. "I was getting our milk for lunch."

Charlie shook his head and gestured with his hands. "I'm sure there was nothing else in the envelope. When I took the card out of the envelope, it was as empty as it is now."

Dr. Dixon clapped his hands. "Okay, let's see what we can do. First, it's obvious that we can rule out that card. Chelsea and I can see no connection. Let's put it away and put our medical knowledge to work in figuring out what this thing is."

The doctor did a routine checkup to check his blood pressure, pulse rate, et cetera "Well, I have never seen or heard anything like this in my life." He scratched the back of his head with his right hand. "Outside of this rather disturbing green, he seems to be quite healthy."

Maggie gestured toward the parlor with her left hand. "Why don't you two and Charlie sit and be comfortable while I get the table set for dinner."

Charles Dixon sat on the cabriole-leg sofa next to his wife. He put his face between his hands and starred silently. Suddenly, he leapt from his seat, grabbed Charlie's arms and held them about ten minutes. Then he gently pulled Charlie into his bedroom, closed the door with his foot, had Charlie take his shirt and pants off, carefully examined him, and shook his head. "I can't find any blotches, rash, or any insect bite."

Charlie's heart fluttered in his chest. "Am I going to die? Is it fatal? Do you know what it is?"

By the time Charlie was dressed, Maggie had joined Chelsea in the parlor. As the doctor and Charlie came back in the room, both women gave the doctor a quizzical look. Charles threw up his arms. "It's beyond my knowledge. Outside of the green, I can't find any rash, any blotches, any insect bites, or anything for that matter to give insight as to what's causing this green. As far as I can see, he's in excellent health. I can find no medical reason for the green. I'm completely bewildered at present."

Charlie scratched the back of his head with his right hand. "But why did you hold my arms so long?"

"I didn't believe that it was contagious, but I had to prove it to myself." He gestured with his hands. "I'm not turning green."

"But why did you shake your head in the other room?"

"No particular reason. This thing has me baffled."

Chelsea handed Charlie his birthday present. "Well, whatever this thing is, there is no reason why we can't still celebrate your birthday. After all, birthdays should be celebrated."

Maggie gave out a laugh and ran to her bedroom. When she returned, she gave her lad a kiss on his forehead. "Chelsea's right. You can open this one too." She paused and motioned toward the kitchen. "However, I think that we should eat our supper before you open the presents. It's been staying warm on the stove a little longer than I like."

Everyone stood up and followed her to the kitchen. Charlie took his seat at one end of the table, while Dr. Dixon and Chelsea sat on a Governor Carver side chair on each side of the table. Maggie placed the pot of corn beef and cabbage along with homemade biscuits on the table. "This may not seem like a grand birthday supper, but this is Charlie's favorite." She gave a little chuckle. "Besides, he's really waiting for his chocolate birthday cake."

Dr. Dixon suddenly took on a puzzled look. "Wait a minute! Where's Toby? Why isn't he here?"

Maggie threw up her arms. "I had to put him in the spare bedroom. He was all frenzied at the sight of Charlie and ran in circles while barking. No matter what I or Charlie said, we couldn't calm him down." She gave out a heavy sigh. "Before you came, I let him out and he seemed to bark louder. You see, Charlie gets a brighter green as the hours go by, so I put him back in the room."

The doctor thought for a moment, got up from his chair, and went to the spare room. He held Toby close and rubbed behind his ears. "Fetch Charlie." Charles had seen Charlie and Toby play hide-and-seek many times.

When Toby found Charlie, he crouched on the floor and kept his distance. Maggie breathed a sigh of relief. "At least he's not barking anymore." She turned her attention to Charlie. "I know this green is difficult, but since your Pa's been gone, you've always given thanks for the evening meal."

Charlie sat up straight with chest out. "Pa wouldn't let any glowing green stop him from being thankful." He bowed his head. "Blessed Savior, I may not understand this green thing, but I do understand that we thank you for this meal and ask your blessing upon it."

"Amen!" Maggie echoed with her lad.

After they finished supper, had a large slice of birthday cake, and everyone helped clear the table, Maggie directed everyone to the parlor. "Let's all go into the parlor, so Charlie can finally open his presents." She paused and gave her lad a hug. "After all, this is supposed to be a birthday celebration."

Everyone laughed as they sat down. Then all eyes were on Charlie who sat on a Queen Anne chair with cabriole-legs. His Mum sat on the one next to him with a little Penguin Table between them. Chelsea handed him their gift. Charlie gasped as he opened the present. "Oh my, this is wonderful! I knew that I needed a new leather hat, but I hated to part with my old one that Pa gave me." He laughed. "I'll just put the old one away for sentimental reasons. I can never throw it away. It was the last birthday present from Pa." He put the hat on and immediately took it off. "Will this green turn the hat green?"

Chelsea smiled, stood up, walked over to him and touched his hand. "What color are your clothes? Did they turn green?"

A flush crept across Charlie's cheeks. "No, and besides Dr. Dixon is convinced that it's not catchy."

Maggie leaned forward. "Okay, let's open the other one. It's getting late and the doctor, his nurse, you, and I have a busy day tomorrow."

Charlie clasped his hands to his chest. "I already know what your present is. I saw you picking out the material and talking to Mr. O'Malley. It's my much-needed Sunday suit."

Maggie reached over and ruffled his hair. "You and your Pa are so much alike. He would've noticed me doing that also. However, you can still open it."

Charlie grinned as he opened it and suddenly slapped his face with both hands. "Oh my, this has to be the best Sunday suit that I've had yet." He got up and gave his mother a hug. "Thanks Mum. I never expected anything this grand. I'll look like an aristocrat when we go to church."

Charlie's countenance suddenly changed, and he grabbed his head with both hands. "I'll never get to wear it. I'm not going any place with this green."

Dr. Dixon jumped up and grabbed both of Charlie's hands. "Believe me, Chelsea and I are going to do some heavy research to find out what this thing is. This is a strange business, and I'll admit we're baffled at present. But we won't rest until we have an answer." He squeezed both of Charlie's hands tighter. "There has to be someone in the medical field who knows about this type of malady. After all, medical science has come a long way in this century; it's never failed us yet. Believe me, we'll find a medical answer." He gave out a sigh. "It may take some time. In the meantime, my lad, you just stay calm until we find the solution."

At that, Toby walked up to Charlie, stood up against his chest, and licked his face. "Thank you so much, you are a true friend," Charlie had to keep back tears as he gave his dog a big hug.

Chelsea came over and took Charlie's right hand and cupped it between both her hands. "You mean too much to us; we can't let you stay in this condition."

Maggie started to cry. "Both of you are the only family that we have. We thank our blessed Savior for you every day."

3

All is Vanity

THERE'S ALWAYS SOMEONE SEEKING to be a mischief maker, and Upton Town has its share. However, Peter Smith is the most notorious of naughtiness in that town. At fifteen, he is completely uneducated. The sad truth is that he could have changed his situation. Father Flanagan offered him a little job, if Peter would allow the priest to teach him how to read and write for a couple of hours a day. Pete would have none of it. Since his parents couldn't read nor write, he felt that there was no need to be educated. His Pa didn't have to read and write in the coal mine, and that's where he would work when he turned sixteen. The lad felt that it was just a waste of his time. Besides, he was having too much fun with his tomfoolery.

All that mattered to Pete was his mischief making. His whole attention was on himself; he was in a world of denial to the needs of others. With six siblings under him ages thirteen, eleven, nine, seven, five, and three, he had no desire to stay around the house. The lad was in a fantasy world and took nothing seriously. Mr. Smith had told Pete that he would get a job in the mine when he turned sixteen, for his Pa wanted to give him some time to be a child. Pete's Pa was put in the mine at eight and never had time to just play. However, Pete has no understanding of the difficulty of working in the mine.

His Pa works in the coal mine six days a week doing twelve hour shifts and is ignorant of the fact that his son is such a town nuisance. It seems that his Mum tried to get him to help her with his siblings, but he skips out the back window right after his Pa goes to work and comes home just before his Pa gets home.

Pete's secret ambition is to get out of poverty and live like Colin Coyle and Charlie McGee with their big houses and land to have a garden. However, the problem with his philosophy is that he hasn't grasped that those two lads are steadfast workers who do all they can to help their widowed Mums. Whereas, Pete has allowed himself to be blind to his Mum's need of help. In his delusional world of self-induced blindness, he cannot see that she works from sun-up to sun-down cooking, cleaning, mending, washing clothes, tending to all the children, and whatever else needs to be done; he has yet to accept the revelation that her work is endless.

If he does do anything for her, it must be something that he wants to do. On this morning, Mrs. Smith was waiting outside the window that he slips out of. At the sight of her, he practically fell out the window. "Mum, whadda ya doin out here?"

She stretched out her right hand holding a piece of paper. "I gotta have this here medicine from da docta. Will ya fetch it fer me?"

He looked at the paper, shook his head and placed it in his satchel. "Ya, I'll fetch it fer ya. But ya know I'll be late gettin home."

She nodded. "Kay, I kin waits."

Peter knew that the doctor and Mrs. Dixon like to sit and have tea in their conservatory built on the back of the house where they grow plants and herbs to make medicine. Whenever he's had to get his Mum's medicine, he would get there early before any patients arrived. Each time, he found the doctor and Mrs. Dixon sipping tea and discussing their day's work.

When he arrived at the doctor's, he just let himself in the front door. Dr. Dixon always unlocks the door early for his patients to come in and take a seat until it's time for his wife to question the purpose for their visit. Sometimes, she can handle the situation without the doctor, which helps them get through the day more easily.

Peter walked in to find the waiting room empty and went to head for the conservatory, but he thought he heard voices coming from the doctor's office. He walked toward the door and heard Mrs. Dixon. "Have you heard back from Dr. Kendall about Charlie's condition?"

At that question, Peter stopped and tiptoed closer to the door to listen. He heard Dr. Dixon ruffling papers. "Yes, here it is. It came late yesterday, and I forgot to tell you with us hurrying to get to that meeting of the New Age of Medical Science Society. Anyway, he has no clue to what Charlie has. He even wrote to Dr. McMann in Bloomfield and he had no idea what Dr. Kendall was talking about. There isn't any information about a glowing green slime disease."

"What are we going to do?"

When Peter heard Mrs. Dixon speak, he thought he heard them start to walk toward the door. At that, he quickly tiptoed out and quietly shut the door. He ran to the side of the house, chest heaving, and tried to calm down, but he was full of questions. "Whatza glowing green slime disease? How'd Charlie git it? Is Charlie gunna die?" He paused and pointed up with his right forefinger. "I'll run ta Olney Junction ta see Colin. Bein Charlie's bes friend, he'll know wut a glowing green slime disease is."

As Peter ran, he thought about how Charlie and Colin were close like brothers. They told everyone that they couldn't have been closer if they were real brothers. Yet, he couldn't understand anyone being close to his brothers. He had five and wanted nothing to do with any of them.

When Pete arrived at Shawn O'Hara's Shoemaker Shop, Colin was busy at work. Shawn noticed Peter Smith standing in the other room and watching Colin. Although he knew that the lad was usually up to no good, he figured he'd let Colin see what he wanted. "Colin," Shawn said, "I think that we'll need additional glue for these shoes. You'll have to get some from the cellar; the supply bucket is empty. At the same time, you can see why Peter is here."

Colin looked up from his work and noticed that Pete was there. "Sure, Mr. O'Hara, I'll get it." He then turned to Pete. "What are you doing here? You know that I don't want to be interrupted when I'm working, unless it's an emergency."

"I gutta tawk ta ya. Itza real mergency."

Colin motioned for Pete to follow him to the cellar. Once they were in the cellar, he turned to look at Pete. "Okay, what's so blooming important that you had to come here?"

Pete proceeded to tell Colin all that he had heard between Dr. Dixon and his wife concerning Charlie. When he finished, he threw up his hands. "Do ya know wut a glowing green slime disease is?"

Colin raised his right hand and stroked his jaw. "I haven't seen Charlie for some time, he sent a note that he wouldn't be at church for a while because of his work and had to cancel our Sunday lunch until things settled down. That's happened a few times before, but this is the longest." He rubbed the back of his neck with his right hand. "Perhaps you misunderstood what the Dixon's were talking about."

A spasm of irritation crossed Pete's face. "I ain't no retod. I wuz right outside da door, and I hurd wut wuz sed."

"Okay, calm down. I'll see if I can visit Charlie after church on Sunday and find out what is what then. In the meantime, I have a job to do."

After Pete left, Colin told Shawn what Pete wanted. "I know Pete's a nuisance, but I am a little confused about Charlie. It's not like him to keep something from me. He always tells me what's going on." He rubbed the back of his neck with his right hand. "I finally finished his Sunday shoes that I promised. I'll deliver them on Sunday after church and try to see him then. Maybe I can find out what this is all about."

ℬᕲ

Charlie really disliked missing Mass all these weeks. It was amazing how Father Flanagan had such a way of making the Bible seem alive. His sermons were enlightening and encouraging. Even the older folks, who avoided church on Sunday before the priest came, couldn't understand why this priest helped them to understand the Bible. It no longer seemed like a foreign language, but one that was full of interesting stories. He told them in such a way that it related to real people like them. Each week, they eagerly waited for Sunday to hear what story that he would tell; church was no longer a dread.

As Charlie sat on a kitchen chair with Toby on the floor next to him, he watched his mother peel potatoes. It was obvious why his Pa fell in love with Maggie Shea. She was a bonny woman at thirty-nine with a flawless complexion, large round green eyes, hair like a raven and as radiant as the morning sun. Maggie was such an energetic woman that his Pa laughed and said that her four foot eleven inches and robust spirit reminded him of the wee people.

His contemplation was interrupted by a knock at the back door. Charlie shot out of his chair with Toby by his side, and they both ran to his room. Charlie went to close the door but turned and whispered to his Mum. "I don't want anyone to see me. I know I probably should see Colin, and he will be the first. But right now, unless it's the Dixon's, I'm not ready to see anyone else."

Maggie motioned with her left hand for him to close his door. Then, she calmly answered the door and found Colin standing there with a blond-haired lad that she recognized as Peter Smith. Colin was the one to speak. "Mrs. McGee, I know that Charlie said he was busy, but it's never been this long. I thought that maybe I could see him today for a bit." He showed her a package. "I told Charlie that I would make him a pair of Sunday shoes in my spare time. Sorry that it took so long, but may I come in and give them to him?"

She starred fingering her silver cross with her left hand. Charlie wasn't up to facing anyone, not even Colin, never mind the naughty Peter Smith. Although she felt sorry for the lad, he's been trouble from the get-go. "I'm truly sorry Colin, but Charlie is not feeling well. Dr. Dixon wants him to stay calm."

"O' ya," laughed Pete. "Did he fall in ta sum glowing green slime pit?"

Maggie gave the lad a stern look. "Peter Smith, do you want me to have a talk with your Pa?"

Pete wasn't bothered by too much, but he knew his Pa wouldn't appreciate him being disrespectful to a woman. "Sorry Mrs. McGee, I wuz jus makin fun."

"Well," Maggie said, "you both will have to leave. Charlie's obeying Dr. Dixon's order to stay calm and that means no company. Now, if you will excuse me, I have things to do."

Colin handed her Charlie's shoes. "Please give these to Charlie and tell him that I'll see him as soon as he's better."

Mrs. McGee took the present. "I'm sure Charlie will be pleased with these, but he really is unable to see anyone at this time."

"I understand," Colin said. "Mrs. McGee, does Father Flanagan know that Charlie's sick?"

Maggie fingered her silver cross with her left hand. "No, I haven't told him."

Colin nodded his head. "Okay, I won't be able to see him until next week at Mass, but I'll light a candle for Charlie and tell the priest that he's not well."

Maggie nodded. "Thank you, Colin."

The lads turned, walked away, and heard the door shut. Pete gave out a laugh. "Let us hide hind that tree."

Colin looked around. "I think the tall grass behind that hill near the barn will keep us from being seen." He motioned with both hands. "What are we hiding for? I have chores to do at home. There are things too heavy for my sister's to take care of, so I help them on Sundays."

Pete laughed. "Don't ya know nuttin? Charlie gut ta do his jobs. Ya know he's like da pony express; nuttin stops him."

Colin folded his arms and starred at Charlie's farmhouse which had always felt warm and full of character. The house seemed to have the same quality as his friend. "I must admit, I am really concerned about Charlie. Besides, I want to know what a glowing green slime disease means."

It was as Pete declared. Charlie was a punctilious lad about duty. Green slime or not, he had the animals to feed, cows to milk, troughs to fill with fresh water, et cetera. They had barely gotten situated when they heard Charlie and Toby. "Well, Toby, let's get our work done while we wait for Dr. and Mrs. Dixon to get here." He scratched the back of his head with his right hand. "I sure hope that they have something positive to report. It's been so long, and I really dislike not seeing Colin. Never mind missing church."

At the sight of Charlie, Colin's hands grabbed his chest as he gasped for air. "This is shocking. I never expected anything like this. He almost doesn't look human. It's like he's not human. I'm quite distressed."

"Kinda looks like da blokes dressed fer da circus," Pete snickered. "Whatza matta, Colin, ya fraid a liddle greeeeeen slime?"

Toby looked in the direction of the hill and started barking. Both boys laid down flat and didn't move.

"It's okay Toby, I don't see anything. It's probably that old jack rabbit that's been running around here lately." He turned to walk away with Toby following him.

"Dat wuz close," Pete whispered.

Colin, a serious-minded lad, peeked up and observed his best friend. There was a kindred spirit between the two. Both were Irish, lost their Pa's, and were devoted to their widowed Mums. They didn't see too much of each other as Charlie had a great responsibility running the farm and Colin had to work in the next county for the shoemaker. At age eleven, Colin had become the masculine influence in his family; this taught him to think rationally.

"Whadya lookin at? Ya gut sumpin ta say?"

"You know that I wanted to see Charlie. However, this seems to be quite serious. It's a ghastly situation."

"Cum offa it. I cum ta hav sum fun, and I'm gunna hav it."

"I don't know if that's wise. Use your head, Pete. What if he's contagious? It looks serious to me. We really should stay away.

Besides, I don't think Charlie wants anyone to see him. You heard him say that he dislikes not seeing me."

"Ya soun like a blinkin coward."

At five foot eleven and brawny build, Colin towered over five-foot four skinny Pete. "I'm no coward, and you know it. Coward or not has no relevance here. It's wisdom that's needed in this situation, and common sense tells me to walk circumspectly and don't be a fool."

"Whadda ya talkin bout? Ya callin me a fool?"

"I'm not calling anyone a fool. I said that we need to use common sense. It's not right to make a joke out of someone else's dilemma." He pointed towards Charlie with his right hand. "This is serious. Besides, Charlie's my best friend, and I don't want to make him uncomfortable. I think he's suffering enough with whatever that disease is."

"Think wat ya want." Pete pointed to himself. "Me, is gunna hav sum fun."

"What if you catch it?"

"Ya gutta be kiddin. Did ya see his Mum? She ain't green. Toby ain't green." He gestured at the animals in the field. "I ain't saw no green cows, green chickens, or green ducks. It ain't catchy, or they wooda been green. Bugga off."

Colin grabbed Pete's arm. "Wait a minute. I thought of something else. What if it's only catchy to those who get him angry? I mean to anyone who gets him blinking mad."

"Whadda ya talkin bout?"

"Mr. O'Hara told me there are supernatural things that we don't understand and know little about. What if something evil is going on?"

Pete's eyes widened. "Are ya talkin bout evil spirits? Kinda like da ol witch in West County castin spells on folks who gut er mad?"

"Exactly! This isn't natural. People don't turn into bright green slime. I just don't think it's safe to get too close."

Pete awkwardly cleared his throat. "Ya jus might be right. I neva thot bout no evil spirits. I ain't no coward, but I no naught bout evil spells."

Colin nodded. "That's what I mean. I don't want to tangle with any evil spirits either. That's a job for Father Flanagan."

ॐ

Shawn O'Hara lives at Olney Junction in Kade County with his elderly mother and his sixteen-year-old niece, Katie O'Hara. He's a bachelor of forty with a solid build gained from hard work since he was about twelve. His parents had him late in life, and his Pa died when Shawn was nineteen. Since that time, he took over the business to take care of his Mum. He did have a brother, Finn, who was eighteen years older. However, Finn was not interested in being a shoemaker and went to Ireland when he was thirty and Shawn was twelve. Ten years later, Finn married an Irish lass ten years his junior. Two years after his marriage, they had Katie who was just six months old when both Finn and his wife died from an influenza epidemic. After her parents' death, she lived with her maternal grandmother until she passed away when Katie was ten. At that time, since Shawn and his mother were her only living relatives, he travelled to Ireland to get her.

Shawn was waiting for Colin to get to work. It's not that Colin is ever late, but he was curious about the story concerning Charlie McGee. Shawn didn't know the McGee's personally, although they all went to St. James Church. Father Flanagan had a seven o'clock and a nine o'clock mass, and they never saw one another. The O'Hara's went to the seven and Maggie and Charlie went to the nine. As soon as Colin walked in the door, Shawn beckoned him into the back room in case a customer came in. "Did you find out about Charlie?"

Colin motioned with both hands. "He has the glowing green slime disease."

Shawn's eyebrows scrunched up. "What in Ireland is a glowing green slime disease?"

"All I can tell you is that he's like a green slimy lantern. He's all lit up and glowing real bright, but it looks like green slime. It's hard to explain. I've never seen anything like it."

"What did the doctor say?"

"I haven't seen Dr. Dixon. I told you that Pete heard him tell his wife he couldn't get any information about a glowing green slime disease." He gave a lethargic motion with his right hand. "Pete and I went to see Charlie yesterday. His Mum won't let anyone see him, but I believe it's because Charlie doesn't want to be seen. Pete and I heard him say that he really disliked not seeing me." He rubbed his temple with his right hand. "We pretended to leave and hid in some tall grass behind a hill near the barn and waited for Charlie to come out and do his chores. It was more horrible than anything I've ever seen. He doesn't even look human. It's like something almost unbelievable if I didn't see him with my own eyes."

"Does anyone know how he caught it?"

"I don't know." He gestured with both hands. "I didn't ask. I was too shocked at what I saw."

Shawn rubbed his left forefinger across his bottom lip. "Well, this is quite baffling." He gestured with his left hand to the other room. "Well, my lad, we have plenty of work to get done. Whatever is going on with Charlie McGee will have to wait until later." He gave a chuckle. "My customers don't like waiting for their shoes."

Colin nodded. "I guess I'll just have to wait until next weekend. Maybe then Charlie might be willing to see me." He paused. "Perhaps, if I tell Mrs. McGee that I already saw Charlie, she may let me in."

"That sounds like a good plan. Now, my plan is to get some shoes repaired, and then we'll start on the new ones for the Thomas family." He chuckled. "My Pa was the only one in the area, until Matthew Jones started his shoemaker business in West County, that could make shoes and repair them. That's why the shop has shoemaker and cobbler on the sign." He sighed. "However, that does make for a lot more work, but I am thankful for the ability and the means to support us." He pointed towards Colin's apron. "Now, let's get going or we'll have some disgruntled customers."

Colin felt his stomach flutter all the way to Charlie's after Sunday Mass. He reached over to rub his horse's neck. "Well, Riley, I sure hope Mrs. McGee lets me in this time. I really want to talk to Charlie and let him know that I don't care what color he is. Father Flanagan taught that friends are not to look on the outside; it's the heart that matters." He gave a heavy sigh. "Charlie has the biggest heart that I know." He paused, raised his right hand and stroked his jaw. "I wonder what Father Flanagan thought when I told him about Charlie. He just stared at me and then said he was busy. The priest doesn't usually rush anyone off." He shook his head. "He must have had something really important to do."

At the sight of Charlie's house, Colin wondered if he was doing the right thing. However, he told Mr. O'Hara that he would try to find out what he could. The lad wasn't one to back out of his promise. With a heavy sigh, he rode around to the back door, tied the reins around the post, walked up to the door, and knocked.

Maggie and Charlie were sitting at the table finishing their lunch. As usual, Charlie bolted to his bedroom with Toby close at his heels while Maggie answered the door. She opened the door and found Colin standing there. "Colin, what are doing here?"

"I'm sorry about last Sunday," he said through a strained voice. "I don't know what I was thinking when I brought Pete with me, but it was Pete who heard Dr. Dixon and Mrs. Dixon talking in their office. They didn't know that he was there, and he snuck out before they saw him." He cleared his throat. "May I please talk to Charlie?"

Maggie stiffened. "Peter heard the doctor and his wife having a private conversation?"

"Yes."

"I don't know what Peter Smith thought he heard, but Charlie's not up to seeing anyone at present. When he's ready, he said to tell you that you will be the first."

Colin rubbed the back of his neck with his right hand. "Mrs. McGee, do you know how Charlie caught the glowing green slime disease? When I saw him, I was too muddled to talk to him. I just want to tell him that I don't care what color he is. He's my best friend."

Mrs. McGee tried to compose herself. "You saw Charlie? When?"

"When he did his chores last Sunday, Pete and I hid. We didn't talk to Charlie, because we didn't know if it was contagious." He gestured at her with his right hand. "But you haven't caught it, so it can't be." He looked into her eyes. "I just need to talk to Charlie and tell him that I don't care what color he is."

"Colin, what can I do? Charlie doesn't know how he caught it and neither do I. The doctor has no idea what the problem is, and he has no idea how to cure it." She gestured with both hands. "All I know is that it's not catchy. I'm sorry, but Charlie is beside himself and isn't ready to see anyone. I must go in. Please don't come back until Charlie sends for you."

Colin hung his head, slowly got on Riley, and rode away.

Maggie watched until he was out of sight and went back into the house.

Charlie gave his Mum a quizzical look. "What did Colin want? I saw him ride away through my bedroom window."

"He wanted to know how you caught the glowing green slime disease and if it's contagious."

Charlie grabbed his head with both hands. "Green slime? How does he know? Who told him?"

"It seems that Peter Smith overheard Dr. Dixon and Chelsea discussing you. They had no idea that he was in another room, and he didn't let them know that he heard them." She fingered her silver cross. "All I know is that he told Colin and they both saw you last Sunday."

"Blessed St. Patrick!" Charlie shouted as he began to pace the room and gesture with both hands. "Isn't anything hidden around here? I must be the talk of the town, the center of every blooming joke." He stopped and looked at his Mum. "You know that if Pete knows, then the whole blooming town has been told. I've got to get away. I have to hide." He grabbed his head with both hands. "I can't go anywhere, who will run the farm? I can't leave you alone. Besides, we haven't found anything to hide this glow. I feel like I sleep with a hundred candles all burning brighter and brighter." He sat on his Governor Carver arm chair and put his chin in his hands. "Mum, what am I going to do? I still keep thinking about Father Flanagan's blessing me on my birthday that turned out to be a nightmare."

Toby barked and went over to where Charlie was sitting and began kissing his hand.

Charlie began to pat his head. "You know Pete Smith too. He's like the worst person that could know. My whole life is ruined."

Maggie placed her right hand on her lad's right shoulder. "We have to be calm. I believe that Father Flanagan's blessing may still prove to be a blessing. Your Pa always said that sometimes a blessing is hiding in adversity." She ruffled his red ringlets. "And don't forget Dr. Dixon and Chelsea are working overtime to get answers. They said they would stop by this afternoon."

"It's almost two blinking months. I glow brighter each day that I'm waiting for them to find a cure. It doesn't make any sense why they can't come up with an answer. They always seemed to have the answers before. All I know is that they've found no cure and this glow is worse each day." He paused and gave a quizzical look. "But I don't think that's what Father Flanagan meant when he said that we should be like a light on hill helping people through the darkness."

"Charlie you must be calm. There must be an explanation. We must be patient. Remember, patience is a virtue. Father Flanagan says that waiting is a difficult thing, but it must be learned."

Charlie stood up and again started pacing the room. "Well, I believe that I know the explanation. I'm bewitched. I don't know how, since I never went near that witch in West County." He stopped and threw his arms up. "I don't even think that I've ever been in West County." He gave a puzzled look. "Have I?"

Maggie shook her head. "Not that I recall. But you really do have to calm down before you cause a complication or something." She grabbed him by his shoulders and looked her lad in the eyes. "Charlie, you can't let this green destroy who you are."

Charlie stared at his Mum and then sat down on a kitchen chair. "Well, now I understand what Father Flanagan meant by saying 'all is vanity.' I had no idea how conceited I was about myself, until I turned green. I was proud of running the farm, taking care of you, and that I was the looking glass image of Pa. Now, I don't even want my best friend to see me."

Maggie sat on the side chair next to her son and fingered her silver cross with her left hand. "Remember, your Pa also said many times that difficulty has a way of making us see truth."

Charlie shot out of his chair. "Pa was so full of wisdom. He would be disappointed in me acting like this. There's no way he would have refused to see Dr. Dixon for any reason." He went to his room and returned with paper and quill. "I'm going to write a note to Colin, ask him to forgive my vanity, and ask him to stop over after church next Sunday." He turned to his Mum. "Will you bring it to his house when you go into town this week?"

Maggie stood up and gave him a hug. "Now, that's your Pa's lad talking."

4

Father Flanagan's Cure

COLIN WAS QUITE DOWN in the dumps as he walked into the shop. Shawn was busy waiting on Mrs. Thomas. She had asked if she could come before hours, as she had to be in West County for an appointment. The sole had come loose on one of her old shoes and she really needed her new ones, while Shawn repaired the old pair. It was imperative that she keep her important engagement.

Shawn was busy helping Mrs. Thomas, and Colin watched the man that he respected like a father. At forty, Shawn was a handsome man. His raven black hair crowned his forehead and exposed rich green eyes. Colin wondered if that's what was meant by the *Emerald Island.* He figured if Shawn was an example of the Irish, then he was glad to be part of this superior race of people. This single man not only supported a ninety-year-old mother and a niece but was a godsend to the Coyle family. As far as Colin was concerned this man was kin to an angel; the man was so selfless.

Shawn had seen Colin come in and tried to hurry Mrs. Thomas along without seeming to be doing so. She no sooner closed the door behind her, when He quickly walked over to Colin. "What did you find out? Did you speak to Charlie or his mother?"

Colin rubbed the back of his neck with his right hand. "I'm afraid that I didn't do too well. No, I didn't see or speak to Charlie, and yes, I did see his mother and talk to her. However, she wouldn't let me see Charlie. She said that he's just not up to seeing anyone at present. How he caught it, no one knows. It seems that it can't be cured, because no one has any idea what he has. The only thing that I do know is that it's not contagious."

ℜ

Father Flanagan was up before dawn on Monday morning. After what Colin had told him, he was quite concerned about Charlie and quickly took care of needed business. When he received the note from the McGee's that they would not be in church for a while, he thought nothing of it. He was used to some of the farmers missing church at certain times, but he was confused that the note didn't mention anything about Charlie being sick. On the way to the McGee farm, he practically ran his horse all the way. When he arrived, Charlie was in the barn and didn't hear him ride up. The priest tied his horse to the front porch column, hurried up the porch steps, and knocked on the door. Maggie was startled by the knock on the front door; she knew that the Dixon's always come to the back door. And it couldn't be Colin who also comes to the back door, besides she hadn't delivered Charlie's note yet. She planned on doing that when she had to go into town tomorrow to get supplies. She wiped the flour from her hands on a towel and answered the door. When she opened it, she was taken aback to see Father Flanagan. "My goodness, Father, what are you doing here?"

Father Flanagan blessed himself. "I beg your pardon Mrs. McGee, but ever since Colin told me about Charlie yesterday, I have been trying to get here. It was just that I had so many prior appointments to keep that this was the earliest I could break away. I was really confused as to why you didn't tell me that Charlie was sick." He took a deep breath and let out a deep sigh. "I really must see Charlie. Perhaps, I can help."

Maggie didn't want to turn this priest away. She was sure Charlie didn't mean him when he said that he didn't want to see anyone. After all, he was ready to see Colin. She stood away from the door and beckoned with her left hand. "Why don't you come in, Charlie will be in about eleven-thirty to get ready for lunch. In the meantime, we can talk." She led him to the kitchen and motioned to a chair. "You have a seat there and I'll get you a cup of tea. While lunch is cooking, I'll join you. Then, you can tell me why you believe that you must see Charlie." She poured the priest and herself a cup a tea and sat down at her end of the table.

The priest took a sip of his tea. "I surely do enjoy a nice cup of tea." He took another sip and began fingering the rosary hanging from his waist with his right hand. "I have to know what a glowing green slime disease is and see if I can help in any way. When did he catch it? There has to be some answer in the Bible." He clasped his hands together. "After all, I do believe that the Bible has the answer to all life's problems. We just have to search for them."

Maggie fingered her silver cross with her left hand. "I'm sorry that we didn't tell you, but Charlie has been beside himself. He hasn't wanted to see anyone, not even Colin." She took a sip of tea. "It seems that Charlie got it right after you left on his birthday. He said that you gave him a blessing and asked our Blessed Savior to bless his birthday as no other."

Father Flanagan leaned back in his chair and blessed himself. "Surely, he doesn't think that I gave it to him? Does he?"

Maggie gasped. "Of course not! It's just that you asked me when he caught it. That's when it happened."

Father Flanagan was telling Maggie how the Bible lists all kinds of diseases and what to do about them. In the Old Testament the priests and prophets handled all types of infirmities. The New Testament talks about laying hands on the sick and praying in the Name of Jesus for healing. They were so engulfed in the conversation that they didn't hear Charlie and Toby come in the back door, until the room was a glowing green.

At the sight of Charlie, the priest blessed himself. "Bless me! I had no idea what it would look like. This is most mind boggling."

Charlie's mouth dropped as he stared at the priest. "Father Flanagan! I didn't know you were here."

Toby went over and licked the priest's left hand.

The priest gazed at Charlie and started to finger the rosary hanging from the belt around his waist with his right hand. "Did anything peculiar happen the day of your birthday? Your Mum said it happened after my blessing, but I wouldn't consider my blessing anything strange."

Charlie gave out a sigh. "Well, I guess there's no need in my hiding." He gestured with his right hand. "Since you're sitting in that chair and looking at me." Charlie quickly went to his bedroom with Toby close at his heels.

Father Flanagan stood up. "I guess I upset him by being here. I meant no harm; it was just that I thought maybe I could help. After all, the priests always helped in the Bible."

Before Maggie could respond, Charlie came out of his room holding the envelope that housed the strange card. "Here," he said as he handed it to the priest. "It happened after I read this peculiar card on my birthday. That's the only unusual thing that happened that day."

Father Flanagan took the card out of the envelope and read the words out loud.

> "Charlie, did ye think ye got away?
> Why did Teague ye disobey?
> Did ye forget the power of old?
> Say not, ye were not told.
> Ye alone chose this fate,
> When friendship ye did abdicate.
> As brother to brother we were,
> Till toward evil, ye did stir.
> Ye took a charm to the green,
> And hid in the night unseen,
> Ye stole what was mine,
> Now green, ye shall shine."

The priest sat back down in his seat and blessed himself. "When did you have any dealings with a Leprechaun?"

Charlie threw his arms up in the air. "A Leprechaun? I've never even seen a Leprechaun, never mind have any dealings with one. What are you talking about?"

Father Flanagan clasped his hands and shook them. "Well, my lad, we know how you caught the glowing green slime disease. A Leprechaun named Teague has used his powers of old for revenge. However, if you've never seen one, I'm a little baffled why this one would want revenge on you."

Charlie slapped his face with both hands. "Wow! Does that mean that you know how to cure me?"

Toby stood on his hind legs and licked the priest's face.

Charlie walked over to the dry sink, poured water from the pitcher into the bowl to wash, and turned to address the priest. "I do believe that Toby has confidence in you to find the answer."

Maggie giggled. "Well, Father Flanagan, it seems that Toby thinks you know how to cure Charlie." She gestured with her left hand. "At present, I think before we continue, it would be beneficial that we eat our lunch. Since it may take time to do all this, I do believe that you should join us." She smiled. "We can discuss things while we eat. Besides, I think that we'll all work much better on a full belly."

Father Flanagan smiled. "You just might be right. I hurried out so fast to do things this morning that I didn't have breakfast. Smelling that food cooking has really worked up a hunger in me." He gestured toward the stove. "I must admit that I am quite hungry."

Charlie laughed. "Well, I know that I'm really hungry. Although I'm eager to get going, my growling stomach is urging me to eat."

Maggie set the food on the table and poured them all a cup of tea. "Now, we can think and satisfy the growling in our bellies."

Everyone laughed, Father Flanagan gave the blessing, and they all proceeded to eat. When they finished, the priest bit the hangnail on his left thumb and gave Toby a pat on his head. "Well, Toby, I don't know what to do at present. Let me sit quietly to think and pray. I'm sure there has to be an answer in the Bible somewhere."

Father Flanagan fingered his rosary with his right hand, stared at the floor for a while, and looked up at Charlie. "Well, the Bible tells of a story in 2 Kings chapter five about a leper by the name of Naaman, a Syrian. In the story, the leper went to the prophet Elisha who told him to wash seven time in the Jordan River."

Maggie fingered her silver cross with her left hand. "But Father, Charlie isn't a leper."

He held up his right hand. "I understand but let me finish. The number seven means perfection."

Maggie shrugged her shoulders. "I'm sorry for interfering. Please continue."

"So, if Charlie can wash himself seven times in water comparable to the Jordan, which to the Syrian was inferior to the rivers of Damascus, that just might be our answer."

Charlie motioned with his hands. "But where will we find water like the Jordan River in Upton Town or in all of Hart County?"

Father Flanagan tapped his lips with his left forefinger. "Um, the only one that I can think of is the Jordon Lake in Kade County. It's definitely inferior when compared to the pristine lakes here in Hart County."

Charlie grabbed his head with both hands. "How am I supposed to get to Kade County without anyone seeing me? I glow brighter than a candle on a candlestick."

Father Flanagan reached into his pocket and pulled out a four-leaf clover wrapped in a piece of clear paper. "I have an idea. Let me put this clover on you and see if the glow comes through." He put it on Charlie's hand and they all watched the glow disappear where the clover was. Father Flanagan clasped his hands and shook them. "Bless the Lord! It doesn't come through."

Maggie screwed up her face. "Where will we ever find enough four-leaf clovers to cover all of him?"

"I don't believe they all have to be four-leaf clover as long as we have this one. After all, four-leaf clovers are quite rare."

"I don't mean to sound disrespectful, but how am I supposed to sew a bunch of clover together to make clothing? They'll break apart."

Charlie put up his right forefinger. "I have an idea. Colin gave me a bucket of glue from Mr. O'Hara to fix things around here. What if we take a bunch of clover and glue them to an old blanket? Then I could put it over my whole body and use a piece of rope to tie it around my waist. Then just make sure the blanket is hanging on the ground to hide any glow from showing."

The priest clasped his hands and shook them. "That's a brilliant idea. That way you'll be able to walk, and your Mum and I could help direct you." He paused. "I believe that as long as each clover is touching in some manner, it will be fine. What I mean is that I don't believe that we have to cover every spot on the blanket. We just need to do a speck of glue in the middle of each clover and make sure it touches another clover. I'm not sure if too much glue will be unsafe."

Maggie nodded her head. "Yes, that makes sense." She gave a sigh, ran into her bedroom, and quickly came out with an old blanket. "Now, all we have to do is get out in the clover patch and get a bunch of clover."

Father Flanagan bit the hangnail on his left thumb. "There seems to be a slight impediment. If we tie the rope around his waist, how will he breathe under the blanket? It's quite a ride to the lake. His air supply will be cut off for too long."

Maggie fingered her silver cross with her left hand. "Dear me, I didn't even think of that in the excitement of hiding the glow."

Charlie jumped up. "I know how I'll breathe. Colin and I used common reeds to see how long we could sit under water in that pond of spring water. The stems are round and hollow. Surely there must be a way to make a hole in the blanket to put the reed in my mouth and place clover around it."

Father Flanagan gestured with both hands. "That's it. We'll put the blanket over him and at his mouth make a small round hole to fit the reed. Once the blanket is ready, we'll put it over him, put the reed in his mouth, and make sure clover is glued on the blanket to cover the reed." He turned to Charlie. "Why don't you and Toby go fetch a few good reeds and we'll see which one works best."

Once Charlie and Toby returned with the reeds, all three took wooden buckets and filled them to the brim with the clover. Charlie got the glue from the barn, held it up, and laughed. "Well, now we better get started gluing."

While Charlie took care of feeding the animals and milking the cows, Maggie and Father Flanagan kept busy gluing the clover on the blanket to make sure each one touched another clover. They completed the blanket just as Charlie said that he was finished with his chores. "Okay," Father Flanagan said, "let's put it over your head, secure the waist, and see what we have."

Maggie and the priest both gave a sigh of relief, and Charlie knew what that meant. "Those sighs mean that you can't see any glow?"

Toby began to bark and run around Charlie.

Father Flanagan clasped his hands and shook them. "Blessed Savior! Yes, there is no glow showing through. Now, we should get your buggy ready, and then we'll cover him in the blanket, and secure the reed." Once the buggy was ready, he again covered Charlie with the blanket and tied the rope around his waist. He then made a small hole at his mouth, placed the reed in through the hole for Charlie to breathe. Once Charlie assured them that he could breathe, the priest glued clover on the blanket to make sure it touched the reed to make sure there was no glow coming through. However, before they continued, Father Flanagan wanted to be sure that Charlie could breathe easily. "Charlie, can you breathe without difficulty?" Charlie nodded with his head. "Then I do believe that we can head for Jordon Lake. I don't expect anyone to be there by the time we get there. It's already dark and it will be quite late.

Maggie and Father Flanagan sat one on each side of him to keep the blanket in place, while Toby jumped in the back and crouched down. "Well, since I know a quick route to the lake, I'll direct Casey," the priest said while taking hold of the reins.

"Is it far?" Maggie asked.

"It'll be about an hour. It's about twenty minutes North of Olney Junction, but it'll be worth the trip."

As they rode there, Charlie was so excited that his stomach felt like it was doing somersaults. "My insides are tumbling all over," he mumbled. "Is it much longer to the lake?"

Father Flanagan chuckled. "We're almost there. Be calm, my lad. Remember patience is a virtue."

When they arrived at Jordon Lake, Father Flanagan and Maggie carefully perused the area to make sure they were alone. "Well," Maggie said, "I don't see any signs of movement."

The priest shook his head. "Neither do I see any signs of life or movement anywhere. Let's get Charlie out of the buggy and into the water."

Charlie almost fell trying to jump out of the buggy. "Am I close to the water?"

The priest guided his left side. "I would say about twenty more steps."

Maggie put her left arm across to stop him. "Wait a minute! We have to take your boots off."

Everyone laughed while Maggie and Father Flanagan each reached under the blanket to keep back as much of the glow as possible and each took one of his boots off.

"Now," Father Flanagan said, "Carefully step into the water and completely immerse seven times."

Toby followed Charlie into the water and swam in circles around him.

Each time he went under, the water was glowing green. When he came up the blanket hid some of it.

Maggie fingered her silver cross with her left hand and Father Flanagan fingered his rosary with his right hand while they watched Charlie bob up and down seven times. When he came up the seventh time, they saw no glow.

Maggie grabbed her silver cross with her left hand. "Father Flanagan! He's not glowing."

The priest clasped his hands and shook them. "Blessed Savior! This is wonderful."

Charlie stepped out, took the blanket off, and walked over to them. "I'm not glowing. Is it gone?"

Maggie lit a candle, put it near him, stared in disbelief, and dropped the candle. Before she could say anything, Father Flanagan blessed himself and uttered. "He's not glowing, but he's still green. I know he dipped seven times, I was counting. This doesn't make any sense. How can the glow be gone, and he still be green?"

Charlie put his right hand on the priest's shoulder. "At least I can stand here, and no one can see me in the dark. Let's get home. Maybe there's something in the Bible that was missed. I mean, after all, it did show you how to take away the horrible glow."

Father Flanagan took Charlie's left hand and cupped it between his two hands. "You're right. The answer has to be in the Bible; I just have to look closer."

Maggie reached into the buggy and pulled out the dry blanket and towels that she had taken. "Here, let's dry off Toby and you dry off. Then wrap yourself in this before you catch your death." Then she grabbed a basket and pulled it out. "I do think that we should all eat these sandwiches and drink the cold tea. It will be too late to make anything when we get back." She giggled. "I figured we'd have to eat something, so I made these roast beef sandwiches."

Charlie gave a heavy sigh. "Thanks, Mum, I am starving. It will be so good to eat in the dark."

The priest laughed. "Well, I think there is enough light from the moon for us to eat. I must agree with Charlie. I am famished. All of this has given me an incredible appetite today."

Toby barked, and Maggie took out a bowl from the basket. "I didn't forget you." She gave the dog his bowl and handed sandwiches and a jug of tea to everyone. Once they all ate, Maggie put everything back into the basket. "Well, I guess that we can get going. It's getting late, and Charlie has some chores to finish before bed."

Toby began to bark and ran to the buggy and back again.

Charlie ran behind Toby to the buggy. "I do believe that he's as excited as me to get home and find out the rest of the cure."

On the way back, Father Flanagan was citing Bible references for healing. "There must be one that will take the green away. I'm really frazzled tonight, but I'll be praying and searching the scriptures until I find the cure."

Charlie touched the priest's arm and gave a smirk. "Father Flanagan, I'm sure green matches my red hair like a Christmas tree with red trimmings, but I trust you to find the answer." He sat back and folded his arm. "All joking aside, I no longer glow. That's a great relief. It's been a real challenge to sleep in a room glowing bright green. It will be great to sleep normally again. Now, I'll just wait until you find the answer in the Bible to make my skin normal."

5

A Logical Explanation

DR. DIXON AND CHELSEA were intense in their research to find a cure for Charlie. They both were staying up late at night searching their medical books, writing letters to their colleagues, and constantly trying to find a cure through their knowledge of science and medicine. Dr. Dixon was certain that there was some scientific answer for this strange phenomenon. "Well, Chelsea, I'm sure there is a logical explanation to this dilemma. All we have to do is keep searching until we find it."

Chelsea inhaled deeply through her nose and exhaled through her mouth. "I'm sure it has to be identified somewhere. Yes, we won't quit. Charlie is depending on us, and we won't let him down. I mean, he is counting on us for the answer. After all, he won't get it anywhere else."

"That's for sure." He scratched the back of his head. "I just wish that we had something positive to tell Charlie tonight when we check in on him. I know that we usually visit on Wednesday, but we can't miss that meeting tomorrow night. Mr. Wright has to be away on Thursday, and Wednesday is his only night to have the meeting." He threw up his hands. "What difference is one day going to make. We've been searching this thing for a few months and have found no solution." He paused and perused the conservatory.

"Maybe we should have been looking for our own cure. With all our medical and scientific knowledge, we should be applying our knowledge. Perhaps, there is something that we can rub on him to take away the green glow." He gestured with his right hand. "We have all these plants and herbs. Surely something can take away the green."

Chelsea rubbed her left forefinger behind her ear. "I think that you're right. After all, we spent all that time in school and now in practical application. Surely, we can find the answer between us." She sat back in her chair. "I was wondering about chlorophyll. You know the green pigment in plants."

"Of course, I know about chlorophyll. But what does that have to do with Charlie?"

"I thought, perhaps, if we mix some olive oil in and put it on Charlie, it would neutralize the glowing green."

Dr. Dixon scratched the back of his head. "It does sound logical. As a matter of fact, it sounds quite brilliant." He gestured with his hands. "What can it hurt? After all, it can't cause any negative reaction." He chuckled. "He can't glow any greener."

"The other thing that I was thinking was salt water. They claim that salt water heals countless infirmities."

Dr Dixon jumped up from his seat. "That's it. We'll get a bunch of green plants and herbs, mash them to get the chlorophyll out and add some olive oil. That way it will be easy to rub all over Charlie, and then have him take a hot salt water bath." He chuckled. "Of course, I'll have to wear rubber gloves, or I'll be green like Charlie." He gestured with his hands. "All joking aside, what can it hurt to try? Besides, any form of scientific healing had to have someone experimenting to find a remedy. We're just as qualified as anyone else."

Charles and Chelsea worked quickly to get the plants, and both used a wooden mortar and pestle to crush the green plants and herbs, put them into an urn, added some olive oil, and covered it with a cloth. Then they gathered plenty of salt. "Well, Chelsea, I do believe that we're ready to visit Charlie."

"I feel like a giddy schoolgirl. This really has me expectant. The way I see it, is if we can tone down the glow that would be great."

Charles scratched the back of his head. "Precisely. You remember, Charlie's mentioned so many times that he is having a difficult time sleeping with that glow lighting up his room."

"Let's get everything in the buggy; Maggie will have supper waiting. We don't want to be late when we stress repeatedly for our patients to be on time for their appointment."

Charles grabbed the bucket of salt. "Boy this is a heavy one, but we want to make sure the water is really salty."

"Okay, I have the urn of chlorophyll." She paused and perused the room. "I do believe that we're ready."

Charles put everything in the back of the buggy, he helped his wife up into the buggy, walked around to his side, took his seat, grabbed the reins, and nodded to his wife. "Walk on, Daisy."

As they pulled up to Charlie's, they gave each other a puzzled look. "Chelsea, I don't see any green glow."

"Charlie must be out back in the barn."

Charles helped his wife down from the buggy. "I have the salt and you have the urn. I guess we're as ready as we'll ever be."

As they went to knock at the back door, Charlie opened it, and Toby ran out to greet them. Charles almost dropped the bucket of salt. "How did you get rid of the glow?"

Maggie came to the door. "Come in and we'll tell you all about it over supper."

Charlie took the urn from Chelsea and gazed at the bucket of salt. "What is this all about?"

Charles laughed. "I guess we'll tell you all about it over supper."

Once everyone was inside, Maggie pointed to the chairs. "Please take your seats and I'll pour the tea." She poured everyone's tea, took her seat, and fingered her silver cross. "Let's see how to start this thing."

Charlie gestured with both hands. "It was Father Flanagan! He found the cure in the Bible." He paused. "Well, it's not the whole cure, but it took the glow away."

Charles eyebrows scrunched together. "What do you mean the Bible gave the cure?"

Maggie leaned forward in her chair. "When Father Flanagan heard about Charlie from Colin on Sunday, he came right here on Monday. He told us about a story in the Bible about a leper that the prophet Elisha told to wash in the Jordan River seven times and was cured."

Chelsea rubbed behind her left ear with her forefinger. "What does that have to with Charlie? He's not a leper. Besides, the Jordan River is nowhere near here."

Maggie motioned for everyone to be quiet. "Let me finish. Anyway, Father Flanagan had a four-leaf clover that hid the glow. We gathered buckets full of clover, glued them to an old blanket, and used a common reed for Charlie to breathe through. We went to the Jordon Lake in Kade County. Charlie dipped seven times, when he finished, the glow was gone. Father Flanagan is now searching the Bible for the answer to turn his skin normal."

Charles scratched the back of head. "Well, whatever the priest believed in the Bible would cure Charlie, there has to be a logical scientific reason for it. If we look at it all rationally, there must have been something in that water."

Chelsea joined in. "Yes, like a mineral or something that accounts for the change." She turned to Maggie. "After all, Bible healings don't happen today, or anyone who reads the Bible would be healed."

Charles laughed. "Yes, and we would be out of a job."

Charlie got up and started to pace back and forth. "I know that it was the Bible that told Father Flanagan what to do." He threw up his hands. "You know that I love and respect both of you, but there's been no medical logic that's changed anything for a few months. Father Flanagan hears about me on Sunday and on Monday he comes." He gestured to himself with both hands. "Look, I'm not glowing anymore."

Maggie stared at her lad. "Charlie your godparents have been doing all that they know to do."

Charlie sat back down. "I know they have, and I appreciate their efforts. All I'm saying is that it was not medical knowledge, but Bible knowledge that took away the glow."

Maggie gestured with both hands. "Right now, let's everyone be calm and eat. This is a meal that I can't leave on the stove too long." She smiled. "Besides, this is the doctor's favorite. I felt to do something special for all your hard work."

Dr. Dixon sat back and gave a slow grin. "It must be fried chicken, scalloped potatoes, spinach salad, and blueberry pie for desert."

"That's correct. I just know how much you love it."

They all ate and had casual conversation. When they finished, Charlie pointed to the bucket and the urn. "We never did find out what that was all about."

Chelsea got up and retrieved the urn. "Well, the glow is gone, but we still have to purge the green. Charles and I have decided to take matters into our own hands using our scientific knowledge to make a remedy." She took the cloth off the urn and handed it to her husband along with rubber gloves. "Charlie, Dr. Dixon will take you into your room and rub this chlorophyll over your body; you can help with the uncomfortable parts. Once it's all rubbed in, you can put on an old pair of bathing trunks. You see, the chlorophyll will stain." She gave out a heavy sigh. "In the meantime, your Mum and I will get the water ready while we're waiting for you, and then we'll have you soak in a hot salt water solution."

Maggie fingered her silver cross. "What is this supposed to do?"

Charles headed toward Charlie's room, paused, and turned toward Maggie. "We believe that the green chlorophyll may counter the green on his skin and the salt water should finish the healing."

Maggie nodded. "Yes, I've heard of the healing properties of salt water." She turned toward Charlie. "This just may be the remedy that turns your skin back."

Charlie sighed and gestured with both hands. "I still think that Father Flanagan will find the answer." He gazed at Dr. Dixon. "But I don't want to be disrespectful, so I'll try this."

Charlie put an old blanket on the floor. "I don't want to stain the wood."

Dr. Dixon nodded. "Good idea. Now, let's get this mixture on."

Charlie laughed. "If the stuff wasn't wet, I couldn't tell what is me and what is the chlorophyll."

After they were sure he was completely covered, he put on his old swimming trunks. As they entered the kitchen, Maggie and Chelsea were coming back into the room with the empty kettles. Charlie sat down on a chair. "Oh yes, Father Flanagan said that this happened because a Leprechaun was angry at his friend for stealing something."

Chelsea grabbed her stomach with both arms. "That priest gets more bizarre every day."

Charles joined in. "I mean really, Charlie, a Leprechaun did that? You have more sense than that. Like I said there has to be a logical explanation." He gestured towards his wife with his right hand. "Chelsea and I are educated and believe me, science holds all the answers to whatever happens."

Charlie felt his nerves tense. "Father Flanagan is the best priest that Upton Town has ever had." He grabbed his head with both hands. "I don't understand why you're both saying negative things about him. He makes the Bible seem so real and the people in it become alive."

Toby got up and licked Charlie's right hand.

Charles scratched the back of his head. "Charlie I believe that this green disease has you too emotional. You really do have to calm down and think rationally." He paused. "Besides, when have we ever failed you? We've always done what we could to help direct you in the right way."

Maggie gestured with her left hand. "I don't mean to sound anxious, but we really don't want the water to get cooled for Charlie's bath."

Charles gave a heavy sigh and followed Charlie into the next room. "Good, let's get this thing moving along."

Charlie got into the wooden tub, and Charles used a bucket to pour the water over his head. After about a half hour, he stopped. "I don't see any more oil, so I believe that I've got the chlorophyll off. However, the skin is still green."

Charlie dried off and put on his clothes. "I told you, Father Flanagan is searching the Bible for the cure."

Maggie looked at her lad as he came back into the kitchen. "There doesn't seem to be any difference. It's still just as green."

Charlie motioned with his right hand. "Like I said, Father Flanagan will find the cure in the Bible." He paused. "Anyway, I just believe that somehow he will be involved in my cure." He gestured with both hands. "It's something that I can't explain, but I have this strong feeling that it does have something to do with a Leprechaun like Father Flanagan said. He's a very wise man in Bible knowledge."

Charles and Chelsea both gazed at each other, but Charles spoke. "Well, Chelsea, we have a busy day tomorrow. I think that we had better head on out."

"Yes, we certainly do. Besides, I'm quite worn out with all this nonsense about Bible cures, Leprechauns, and ridiculous priests."

Charles retrieved the bucket that had the salt, and Chelsea grabbed the urn that had the chlorophyll. They nodded to each other and walked out.

Maggie, Charlie, and Toby walked out with them.

Chelsea gave Maggie a hug. "Well, we'll just keep working at it. You'll see, the priest has no medical or scientific knowledge, we'll find the scientific explanation."

Charles helped his wife into the buggy. "Chelsea and I will find the scientific reason for the glow disappearing. The priest is an okay man, but he is not a doctor or a scientist. I am convinced that we'll find a medical remedy to take away the green color. Just have to search deeper."

Maggie fingered her silver cross. "Thank you for trying tonight."

Charlie gestured with his hands. "I'm telling you the answer is not in medical science. After all, it wasn't science that took away the glow and you have been trying for months. You must trust Father Flanagan. I know the answer will somehow come from him."

Toby began to bark, hopping on his hind legs.

Charles took the reins. "Walk on, Daisy"

Everyone waved, and Maggie, Charlie, and Toby went back into the house.

Charlie was the first to speak. "Did Pa know that Dr. Dixon doesn't believe in the Bible?"

Maggie fingered her silver cross. "I don't think any of us knew anything until tonight. I'm just as surprised as you." She poured them both a cup of tea. "Let's just sit, relax, and enjoy this tea."

Charlie shook his head. "But I must say that I'm stunned how you can know someone for your whole life and not really know what they believe. This is most shocking to me." He threw up both hands. "I mean the things that Mrs. Dixon said about Father Flanagan. Then Dr. Dixon insinuating that they have the knowledge and that Father Flanagan is stupid because he is not educated in medical science." He grabbed his head with both hands. "I mean they believe they're the only ones with any knowledge and everybody else is stupid."

Maggie sighed. "I'm just baffled that I never saw any of it before tonight. This is quite mind boggling."

Charlie grabbed his head with his hands. "Did you get the note to Colin?"

"I went this afternoon when I picked up some supplies."

Charlie took a sip of tea. "I sure hope Colin doesn't turn out to be like Dr. and Mrs. Dixon when I tell him what happened."

℘

When Colin had gotten home Tuesday night, Mrs. Coyle handed him the note from Charlie. "Mrs. McGee delivered this and asked me to give it to you."

Colin opened the note and his face beamed. "Charlie wants to see me Sunday after Church." He sat heavily into a chair. "But that's five days away."

"Yes, luv, but he wants to see you. That's the important thing." She put her right hand on her lad's shoulder. "It's been a few months." She gestured with both hands. "But surely you can wait a few more days."

Colin raised his right hand and stroked his jaw. "But what does he mean about his vanity? Well, at least I can tell Mr. O'Hara that Charlie wants me to visit." He paused and folded his arms. "The strangest thing happened this afternoon when Mr. O'Hara's niece Katie brought in our lunch. We were talking about the glowing green slime, and she gave a start like she knew what it was or something."

"Did you ask Mr. O'Hara about it?"

"I asked him after she left the room, and he just shrugged it off."

Mrs. Coyle brushed her red hair away from her face with her fingers. "It could just be hearing about glowing green slime. I know I was taken aback when you told me."

"Yes, Mum, you could be right. I sure remember what happened to me when I saw it."

"Right now, my lad, you need to wash up for supper, five in the morning comes pretty fast."

Colin walked over to the pitcher and bowl on the dry sink and poured water into the bowl to wash up. "I know that I get pretty tired." He gestured with his hands. "How Charlie puts in the hours that he does working that farm is beyond me."

"What about his Mum? She doesn't have any daughters to help her with the house and all. I know how difficult it was for me before your sisters were old enough to help, and I didn't have a farm to help run. Mrs. McGee makes all her own butter, cheese, and helps Charlie do the planting and harvesting. Besides all the cleaning, cooking, washing and all, she makes all their clothes." She gave out a heavy sigh. "Maggie McGee is an incredible woman raising an incredible lad." She ruffled Colin's hair. "But my lad is no less remarkable taking on the responsibility to support us since his Pa died."

"I know Mum, but it's really Mr. O'Hara that deserves the credit. What man takes on an eleven-year-old lad who doesn't know anything about being a shoemaker? He not only taught me the business, but also helped school me in arithmetic and such because I couldn't get any more schooling." He raised his right hand and stroked his jaw. "Plus, he paid me a man's wage to support us and even kept us all in shoes." He paused. "And don't forget that he gave me Riley, so I don't have to walk to work. It sure does make it easier riding that horse when the weather's bad."

"You are right, but you still had to be willing to get up at five, six days a week, be at work by seven, work until six, and travel through rain, snow, and sleet."

Colin nodded his head. "Yes, but Charlie can work more than fourteen hours a day depending upon the time of the year, plus he still has to feed the animals and milk the cows on Sunday." He sat down to eat his supper. "I am really looking forward to Sunday. I believe that Charlie and I are closer than brothers like that story Father Flanagan told a while ago about David and Jonathan."

ℛ

Charles and Chelsea sat quietly on their way home. Once home, they emptied the buggy and Charles took care of Daisy. When he finished and entered the house, Chelsea had a pot of tea ready. "I thought that we might just sit and have a nice cup of chamomile tea with a little mint."

"That's a great idea. I feel a little tense after tonight. It seems that this glowing green slime disease has gone to Charlie's head."

Chelsea poured the tea. "I had no idea the lad was so brainwashed by that priest." She sat down. "Don't get me wrong, he is a nice enough individual. But to take him seriously about the Bible is ludicrous."

Charles scratched the back of his head. "I'm truly concerned about the lad. It's obvious that there had to be something in that water." He paused and stared off. "But the priest saying a Leprechaun made him green, I mean how ridiculous." He chuckled. "I think being Irish has that priest's mind green."

"I know what you mean. He's definitely not in a right frame of mind." She took sip of tea. "But I must admit that I was really surprised that Maggie seemed to believe the priest helped. Then the nonsense about the Leprechaun had me in stitches." She paused. "I mean, Charles, Maggie doesn't have the glowing green slime disease. Yet, she seemed to agree with everything Charlie said about that absurd priest."

"The thing that boggles my mind is that I never caught anything like that from them before." He sat back in his chair. "I do believe that confounded priest has them hypnotized or something. We really have to get them to see that there has to be a scientific explanation for what happened." He let out a heavy sigh. "I can't remember a time that they didn't look to us for advice, and now to believe that priest who knows nothing about medical science." He threw up his arms. "This whole thing is a nightmare with that absurd priest and his nonsense."

She rubbed the back of her ear with her left forefinger. Once we find the truth for his so-called miraculous healing, they'll be back to normal." She took a sip of tea and suddenly put the cup down. "Perhaps we should get some samples of that water and check it out for ourselves."

"I think that's exactly what we'll do after work on Thursday. With our work load tomorrow and that meeting tomorrow night, I cannot see us getting there earlier than that." He rubbed his temple with the fingers of his right hand. "We'll prove there's a scientific reason for the priest's so-called miraculous cure."

They gave each other an arrogant grin.

Colin whistled all the way to work on Wednesday morning. He didn't even mind the pouring rain. As soon as he arrived at work, he put Riley in the barn, dried the horse off, put a blanket over him, and made sure he had fresh hay and water. When he walked into the shop, Shawn O'Hara took his rain gear in his right hand, handed him a towel with his left hand, and hung up the rain gear. "Well, Colin, my lad you seem to be quite cheerful today." He combed his hair back with the fingers of his left hand. "Something must have happened. You sure have been in a low countenance lately."

Colin finished drying his face and hands. "I have some great news. When I got home last night, my Mum had a note for me from Charlie." His voice became bubbly. "Charlie wants me to visit after church on Sunday." He raised his right hand and stroked his jaw. "I don't know what happened for Charlie to change his mind, but I'm sure pleased about it. He's never treated me like anything less than a brother. This thing must have been more awful on him than we can even imagine."

Shawn rubbed his left forefinger across his bottom lip. "This is great news. It looks as if we might finally get some answers."

"Yes, I'm sure Charlie will tell me everything." He put his shoemaker apron on. "The main thing is that he wants me to visit, and that he doesn't mind me seeing him."

Shawn put his right hand on Colin's shoulder. "I'm glad that he wants to see you. I believe that it's been difficult on him not wanting anyone to see him." Shawn gave a heavy sigh. "Whew! I can't imagine looking like glowing green slime. I'm not sure that I would be too eager for people to see me."

⋳⋼

Charles and Chelsea were relieved that they had a rather easy day on Thursday and were eager to get a sample of the water from Jordon Lake. They took enough jugs to retrieve the water and rode out to the Lake. They took out the jugs and headed down to the water. "Well, Chelsea, I think we'll soon solve the riddle of the Bible cure."

Once they filled all the jugs, Chelsea gave a smirk. "I do believe that we'll have our answer as soon as we test this water." She paused. "I can hardly wait to get started. We really have to put an end to that priest's control over our godson."

They put the jugs in the buggy, Charles helped Chelsea up, and he climbed up on his side. They both got comfortable and headed back. On their way home, Chelsea gave her husband's left arm a gentle squeeze. "I'm still surprised and overwhelmed at Maggie allowing Charlie to say such rubbish. I really thought she was more level headed. However, like I said, that priest has them brainwashed. It's the only thing that makes sense." She grabbed her husband's left arm tightly. "I mean, really, Maggie and Charlie believing him and not us. We're the ones who have studied medical science and not that stupid priest and his Bible garbage."

His voice shook. "B-believe me, I'm just as shocked as you. This has me quite weighed down." He took a deep breath through his nose and let out a heavy sigh through his mouth. "I'll just be delighted when we prove the scientific explanation for the sudden cure."

As they talked about finding a scientific explanation to prove the priest wrong, they became quite jovial. Charles started to whistle, and Chelsea joined in. "Chelsea, I'm sure glad that you aren't simple minded like that Maggie McGee. I'm surprised that we never saw it before."

"That's not all; it doesn't seem that Charlie is anything like Rory. I don't remember Rory ever talking such nonsense." She turned toward her husband. "Do you?"

Charles scratched the back of his head. "Rory was always more serious than me, but we really didn't see much of each other after I started college. Then, when we were trying to get the practice going, we only saw them on Sunday night for supper." His eyebrows scrunched together. "As a matter of fact, even as lads, we only had Sunday afternoon. He was so busy on the farm with his Pa, and I had to help my Pa with his basket weaving." He stared ahead. "Now, that you mention it, I think that he may have believed the Bible. After Mass, he would bring up what Father Flanagan had said. I just never paid any attention to it." He gestured with his hand. "Perhaps, I should have listened closer. Maybe that's why

Charlie and Maggie believe the Bible is true. You know that all they talk about is how Rory said this or Rory said that." He paused and turned toward his wife. "I'm beginning to think that perhaps it was Rory that started this whole nonsense. Unless, we can prove to them the Bible's a bunch of fairy tales, we may have to forget about being godparents. I certainly can't take much more of miraculous cures, Bible stories, Leprechauns, that dim-witted priest, and the like."

Chelsea rubbed behind her left ear with her left forefinger. "Charles, I have an idea."

"Yes, my dear."

"What if we start going to Mass in West County? Father Wilson seems to be more down to earth than that bizarre Father Flanagan. If we take the back route, it's only about twenty minutes farther from our house than St. James. I'm beginning to sense that we are going to clash with Father Flanagan and his lack of common sense."

Charles stared ahead. "I've been considering the same thing. I don't know how much longer that I can hear the lunacy of that priest and remain silent." He turned to look at his wife. "I mean after all, Charlie is our godchild, and I promised Rory to look after the lad if anything ever happened." He took on a haunted look. "Of course, I never expected anything to happen to Rory. Besides, now I'm not sure if being godparents was a good idea. We really should have paid more attention to what Rory believed." His eyebrows scrunched together. "Now that I think about it, he did always give thanks at meals. I just felt it was a habit that he picked up from his Pa, and Charlie picked up the habit from Rory. Nevertheless, I believe if we can't convince Maggie and Charlie that the Bible is just myths and fairy tales, we're not going to continue any further communication with them. I will not be badgered with Bible cures, Leprechauns, that stupid priest, and thinking all his outlandish Bible stories are true." He paused. "Well, we're here, let's get our samples. The sooner we can prove that priest wrong, the better I'll feel."

Chelsea nodded. "This is so sad, but I have to agree. If they believe him and not us, we'll have no choice." She slapped her thighs. "Well, once we prove the priest wrong with his cure, we'll be able to stir them back on the right path."

They spent every spare moment for the next few days trying to find a significant difference in the water from Jordon Lake and the water from Upton Lake. "Charles, I'm really confused. Outside of Jordon's water being inferior, we've found nothing to account for the glow to disappear."

"Wait a minute! If there's no difference in the water, it's just that it was time for the glow to disappear."

Chelsea gestured with her hands. "Exactly, just like the blisters from chicken pox and the like. They all fade away."

Charles nodded. "I knew there was a concrete science-based explanation."

"I believe that perhaps the green will just disappear when he's completely healed."

"Yes, my dear, you're right." He sat down. "However, unless we can prove it, Charlie will never be convinced. He is totally brainwashed by that priest and his nonsense. Maybe, we had better do what I said and forget about being godparents."

"I know you're right." She paused. "There's no way I want to hear any more about that priest and his Bible." She shook her head. "I'm just dumbfounded that they could turn on us like that and believe that ridiculous priest. I mean, really, Charles, we're the ones with knowledge, not him."

Charles scratched the back of his head. "I don't know if you noticed that Morgan boy. He just turned three and lost his parents a couple of months ago. Maybe we should take him under our wings. After all, he doesn't go to Mass, so that priest has no influence over him."

Chelsea patted her husband's left hand. "Yes, I've watched him when his aunt brings him in. He seems so misplaced." She paused. "But I must admit that she has her hands full with her four young children under six."

Charles sat back and folded his arms. "Do you think that we should adopt him? He's young enough that we can bring him up properly. We could offer his aunt compensation for her to let us take him as our own lad. I know that she and her husband could use the money."

Chelsea grabbed her husband's left hand with both hands. "I don't believe that it will take too much convincing, but I do think that we could make it well worth her while." She paused. "Yes. It's quite obvious that she has him because she's his only living relative, but she's not too pleased with the situation."

"Let's not put it off. I think that we should give Mrs. Cane a visit right now. I do believe that she will jump at the money and the opportunity to free herself of the lad."

Chelsea clutched her chest with both hands. "Oh, Charles, I feel like I'm finally going to give birth to our lad."

"Yes, and we'll make sure that Father Wilson re-christens him as John Henry Dixon; John after my Pa and Henry after your Pa. I just don't want to have another Charlie after what we've been through. If I could, I would take back the name." He sighed. "At least we'll have no more dealings with Father Flanagan and his shenanigans."

They both laughed and hurried out the door to visit Mrs. Cane.

6

Brotherly Friendship

COLIN COULD FEEL HIS pulse beat faster the closer he got to Charlie's house. He was trying to convince himself to be normal and act as if Charlie looked the same. Of course, the glowing green had taken him by surprise, but he wasn't going to let color or glow interfere with him and Charlie. Colin rubbed his horse's neck. "Okay, Riley, we're almost there. We just have to make sure that we don't let Charlie think that the green glow has any effect on our brotherly friendship." He looked up and realized they were there. "Oh, my, Riley, we're here. I'll just take you to the barn to get some fresh hay and water like old times."

Before Colin could finish, Charlie and Toby had come into the barn unnoticed by Colin. When Colin turned around, he dropped the bucket that he was using to give Riley fresh water from the well. "Blessed St. Patrick! Charlie you're not glowing."

Before Charlie could answer, Toby jumped up on Colin and was licking his face. Colin grabbed the dog with both hands and hugged him. "I sure have missed you too."

Charlie laughed. "Okay, Toby, Colin and I have some catching up to do." He grabbed both of Colin's hands. "I'm so wretched for being so vain. Father Flanagan said that vanity can be a flaw and the person isn't even aware of it. I can't believe that I was that conceited." He stood back and gestured with his hands. "It took this green to make me see my hidden flaw. To think that I wouldn't even let my best friend see me. Can you forgive my vanity?"

Colin gave a slow grin and gestured with hands. "To be honest, I don't know how I would have reacted if I suddenly found myself looking like glowing green slime. There's no problem in forgiving you. I'll admit it was hard not having our Sunday visit." He raised his right hand and stroked his jaw. "But I really would like to know how it all happened." He gestured with his right hand. "How did you get rid of the glow?"

"I think you had better come in for lunch. Mum has it prepared. It's all a very long story, and besides my Mum wants to see you too." He picked up the bucket that Colin had dropped, and they headed for the barn doors. "You head on in the house, I'll close the doors, and return this bucket to the well. Besides, I told you, my Mum wants to see you."

Colin walked up to the back door, and Maggie opened it before he reached the steps. "Colin, I am so sorry for how I treated you. But Charlie was beside himself and if truth be told, so was I." She gave him a hug and motioned with her left hand. "Come on in and wash for lunch." She went to close the door, but Charlie was right behind them. "Good, you both can wash for lunch."

Maggie put the food on the table, while the boys washed their hands. "Okay, Colin you sit in your usual seat, and we'll eat."

Charlie gave his Mum a hug. "Thanks, Mum, I'm really hungry." He took his seat. "Colin has a lot to hear about." He jumped up, ran to his room with Toby at his heels." He stopped and patted Toby's head. "It's okay, Toby, we're not hiding anymore." Toby went back to sit near Charlie's seat, while Charlie went into his room. He quickly returned with an envelope and handed it to Colin. "That's how it all began. After you read the card, we'll start the story."

Colin took the card out of the envelope and read aloud.

> *"Charlie, did ye think ye got away?*
> *Why did Teague ye disobey?*
> *Did ye forget the power of old?*

Say not, ye were not told.
Ye alone chose this fate,
When friendship ye did abdicate.
As brother to brother we were,
Till Toward evil, ye did stir.
Ye took a charm to the green,
And hid in the night unseen.
Ye stole what was mine,
Now green, ye shall shine."

Colin fell backward in his chair. "W-when did you see a Leprechaun? You never told me about meeting and being friends with a Leprechaun."

Charlie gave a belly laugh. "Colin, I've never seen a Leprechaun." He gestured toward his Mum. "That's what had us so puzzled."

Maggie gestured with her hands. "As a matter of fact, we had no idea that it was a Leprechaun until Father Flanagan read the card last Monday."

Charlie gave his friend a puzzled gaze. "Wait a minute! How did you know it was a Leprechaun?"

"Mr. O'Hara and his niece Katie told me about them. It seems that Katie has knowledge about them from when she lived with her grandmother in Ireland. They mentioned that Leprechauns have the power of old." He shrugged with his shoulders and gestured with his hands. "So, when I read the power of old, I guess Leprechaun came to my mind."

Maggie fingered her silver cross with her left hand. "Well, after Charlie read that card, he was a glowing green."

"I didn't even realize that I was glowing green, until Mum turned to look at me and stood stone still. She scared me half to death. I thought she was sick or something until I looked in the looking glass. I tried to wash it off, but it kept glowing brighter. And the longer I was green, the brighter and brighter the glow became. It was most frightening."

Colin gestured with his hands. "But how did the glow go away?"

Charlie beamed. "It was Father Flanagan. He found something in the Bible about a leper and the Jordan River, and it worked."

"Wait a minute! First, you're not a leper and the Jordan River is in Israel or near it." Colin's eyebrows scrunched. "This isn't making any sense."

Maggie motioned with her hands. "Let Charlie finish the story. We were just as confused when Father Flanagan first told us the story about a leper. It made no sense to us either."

Charlie continued his story. "What Father Flanagan said is that the leper washed in the Jordan River seven times." He leaned forward. "You see, the number seven means perfection. So, we had to find water that was poor quality like the Jordan River." He gestured with his hands. "The only one that came to Father Flanagan's mind was the Jordon Lake in Kade County."

"You mean you went to Kade County all lit up like that?"

Charlie grabbed his head with his hands. "No, Father Flanagan had a four-leaf clover and it hid the green on the spot that he placed it. So, we got a bunch of clover and glued them to a blanket and I used a common reed through a hole to breathe." He gestured to his Mum. "Mum was beside herself as to where we would find enough four-leaf clovers and how she would ever sew them together. But Father Flanagan said that the one four-leaf was enough. I came up with the idea to use an old blanket and apply the glue you gave me from Mr. O'Hara to glue them to the blanket."

"Wow! I wish I could have seen all that." He gestured with his right hand. "But never mind that. What happened next?"

"We went to Jordon Lake, and I dipped completely in the water seven times with Toby swimming in circles around me to encourage me. When I stood up after the seventh dip, the glow was gone." He sat back and folded his arms. "Father Flanagan is incredible with his Bible knowledge. You told him about me on Sunday. He comes on Monday and the glow is gone. He's busy studying the Bible to find a cure for the green skin."

Colin rubbed the back of his neck with his right hand. "My Mum says that Father Flanagan is the best priest she's ever heard. She's from North County, and she said no priest ever talked about the Bible like he does." He raised his right hand and stroked his jaw. "I must admit I do enjoy hearing his Bible stories. As a matter of fact, he told a story the first week that you missed Mass about David and Jonathan who were closer than brothers. When he told it, I thought that you and I have such a brotherly friendship. However, it sure was difficult what happened after you turned green." He gestured with his hands. "I must admit that I don't know how I would've responded if I found myself glowing green like that." He paused, and his eyebrows scrunched together. "Charlie, do you mind if I tell Mr. O'Hara everything that took place? I mean, how Father Flanagan knew that it was a Leprechaun that sent the card and how he found the cure in the Bible? I told you that I believe that his niece has knowledge of Leprechauns."

"I have no problem with Mr. O'Hara knowing." He gestured with his right hand. "Since Peter Smith knows, I'm sure the whole blooming town knows about it."

Colin's face flushed. "I am so sorry for coming here with him. It was just that I was shocked when he told me what he heard the Dixon's say about a glowing green slime disease." He crumpled in his seat. "I should never have let him come with me. I'm the one who needs to be forgiven."

Maggie patted his right hand. "It's okay. I think that none of us was thinking properly at the time. I know that Charlie's still green, but he's confident that Father Flanagan will be the means to his becoming normal again. I must agree with him." She gestured with both hands. "After all, no one else had any answers. I think the Bible is the answer to all life's problems, if we'll just search and believe."

Charlie threw up his hands. "Yes, I do believe that too. I read a story in the Bible last night about a guy named Joseph. His brothers hated him, put him in a pit, and sold him into slavery. He was bought as a slave by some guy in Egypt, and then he was put into prison because the guy's wife lied. Then years later because of a famine, his brothers come to Egypt and are afraid when they find that Joseph is still alive." He motioned with his hands. "The best part of the story is when Joseph said that what was done to him was meant for evil, but God meant it for good. I truly believe that God was telling me through that story that this thing was meant for evil, but God is going to make it be for my good."

Colin leaned forward in his chair and clasped his hands. "This is exciting. I'm going to start reading our family Bible. No wonder Father Flanagan gets so thrilled about the stories."

Maggie fingered her silver cross with her left hand. "I just don't know why we never read our Bibles before. Instead of waiting to hear a story from Father Flanagan on Sunday, we can read lots of stories all week."

They finished their lunch topped off with a slice of apple pie. Charlie got up to start clearing the table and Colin joined in. "Okay, boys, I can take care of the cleaning. It's a nice day for a swim in that pleasant pond of cool water." She ruffled Charlie's red ringlets. "If your Pa was here, he'd be on his way there." She took on a haunted look. "He truly enjoyed that spring of cool water."

Charlie turned to Colin. "I have extra swimming shorts. What do you say? Shall we go for a swim?"

"You don't have to ask me twice. I'm always ready for a swim on a hot day like today."

When the boys and Toby got back from their swim, Dr. Dixon's cleaning lass was heading for town. They went around to the back door and let themselves into the kitchen where Maggie was peeling potatoes for supper. "Mum, what did Dr. Dixon's cleaning lass want?"

Maggie pointed to a note on the table. "She brought that."

Charlie picked it up and read it. "That's strange. When have they been too busy to come on a Sunday night for supper?"

Maggie fingered her silver cross with her left hand. "To be honest, I was sort of dreading having them here after last Sunday."

Colin gave Charlie a quizzical gaze and Charlie motioned with his right hand. "It's more of the story that we didn't tell you earlier."

Maggie got up and gave both boys a towel. "Why don't you two dry up and get changed? I'll make us a pot of tea and we can tell Colin the rest of the story."

The boys took the towels, hurried to change, and quickly returned. Maggie laughed. "I don't know if you two broke some kind of record for a quick change." She pointed to the chairs. "Have a seat, I'll pour the tea and Charlie can tell the rest of the story."

Charlie sat down and waited for Colin and his Mum to sit. "Okay, we're still trying to get over it. When we told Dr. and Mrs. Dixon that Father Flanagan found the cure in the Bible, they laughed."

Maggie interjected. "Mrs. Dixon said that if that was true then all people who read the Bible would get healed. Then, Dr. Dixon laughed and said that it would put them out of a job."

Colin sat back in his chair and folded his arms. "I had no idea that they didn't believe the Bible."

Charlie continued. "Mrs. Dixon laughed so hard when I told them that Father Flanagan said that a Leprechaun is the cause of the green that she had to hold her stomach with both arms. Then to top it off, Dr. Dixon insinuated that Father Flanagan had lost his mind by what he said to me and that I needed to think more rationally."

Maggie fingered her silver cross. "Colin, like Charlie said after they left on Tuesday, I guess you can know people for years and not really know them." She pointed to Charlie. "My Mum always said the proof is in the pudding, and Charlie's glow being gone is all the proof that I need."

Colin sat back and folded his arms. "Well, now I know why Mr. O'Hara has the doctor from West County treat his mother. He told me that it wasn't that he didn't like Dr. Dixon, but he just didn't get the right feeling from him." Colin shrugged his shoulders. "I just assumed it was because Dr. Dixon is much younger than Dr. Meadows and Mr. O'Hara's mother was more at ease with an older doctor."

Charlie grabbed his head with both hands. "All of this has me baffled. I'm in a straight. It's like they're two strangers, and I've known them my whole life." He turned to his Mum. "I have to admit that I was hoping that they wouldn't come tonight and ruin my good day with Colin."

Colin finished his tea and stood up. "I really do have to go home. There are some things that I have to do for my sisters that they can't do." He raised his right hand and stroked his jaw. "Although I would like to stay and talk some more about all this, I must get home and help them."

Maggie got up and gave the lad a hug. "Colin, I wouldn't expect anything less of you, and I believe that's why you and Charlie have a brotherly friendship."

After Colin left, Charlie sat down at the kitchen table. "Oh, Mum, thank God that Colin isn't like Dr. Dixon." He sat back and folded his arms. "I don't believe that Pa would have named me Charles Dixon McGee if he knew that all this would happen." He grabbed his head with both hands. "I truly wish that he had named me Rory Finn McGee after himself." He slouched in his chair. "It seems that I'm not a Charlie but a Rory."

Maggie cupped his face with her hands. "Charlie, a name doesn't make the person, but the person can make the name."

Charlie gave her a quizzical gaze. "What does that mean?"

"Someone can be named Rory and dishonor the name by his life; whereas, someone else named Rory can honor the name like your Pa did. Dr. Dixon has let you down, but it has nothing to do with the name. You can make your Pa proud that he named you Charles Dixon McGee by you honoring the name by your life."

Charlie got up and gave his Mum a hug. "I think Pa's wisdom has rubbed off on you."

Maggie fingered her silver cross. "I do believe that a lot of your Pa's wisdom came from him believing the sermons that Father Flanagan gave. That's why we must listen to Father Flanagan, because we have a lot to learn."

Charlie nodded. "He's really got a lot of Bible knowledge that's for sure."

Father Flanagan was busy cleaning the altar area to get everything ready for next week's Mass when he turned around and found Peter Smith standing behind him. "W-why, Peter Smith, what are you doing here at this time of night?"

Pete looked down and shuffled his feet. "Ya know that I ben workin in that there mine fer a about a month?"

"Yes, I know. Is there something wrong?"

Pete sat in a pew and gazed up at the priest. "Father Flanagan, I wuz awful wrong. I should a lisened ta ya bout readin an writin." His eyes filled with tears. "I dun know how me Pa is worked all these years in that there mine. It's nuttin like what I thot it wuz." He rubbed his hands down his pant legs. "I jus wish I would a takin the job when ya did ask me. Me Pa sed if'n ya kin pay me wut I get a week, I kin work fer ya." He gazed up at the altar. "I want ta learn how ta be smart like Colin and Charlie. Will ya still learn me?"

Father Flanagan clasped his hands and shook them. "Peter Smith, this is great news." He blessed himself. "I thank the blessed Savior for you finally growing up to truth."

"I jus wish I would a learnt it fer I went in ta that there mine. It's like afta I saw me Pa work, I saw wut me Ma duz. They both jus work an work. I jus feel so bad fer not helpin her when she did ask me ta."

"Yes, but sometimes we learn the hard way. Let's pray that you won't have to learn the hard way again."

Pete blew a heavy sigh. "I sure wuz dum."

Father Flanagan put out his right hand. "Let's shake on our agreement." He took Pete's right hand and gave it a good shake. "I'll tell you what, you can tell your Pa that I'll give you double what you make in the mine." He pointed his right forefinger at the lad. "There's only one condition, you have to be serious about learning how to read and write."

Pete forgot himself and jumped up and hugged the priest. "Thank ya much. Wait ta me Pa hears." He let go of the priest. "Father Flanagan, I promus ta be serious. Ya will see."

"Well, my lad, I think you had better get home. I'll expect you here tomorrow morning at eight sharp. You'll work until noon and have lunch. Then you'll study from one until three and then work until six." He gestured with his hands. "I don't expect you to be late. And when I'm not here, I expect you to do whatever cleaning needs to be done, whether the church or the grounds. Do you understand?"

"Father Flanagan, I promus ta make ya proud."

"Okay, then I'll see you at eight in the morning."

Colin felt cheerful as he rode to work on Monday. He rubbed Riley's neck. "I can't wait to tell Mr. O'Hara all that took place yesterday." He paused to get more comfortable on the horse. "The only thing is where to begin. There's so much to tell, and I don't want to leave anything out."

Shawn could tell that Colin was beaming. "How did it go yesterday at Charlie's?" He gave a grin. "By your countenance, it seems that it went quite well."

"Mr. O'Hara, I don't even know where to start. Charlie gave me permission to tell you everything." He raised his right hand and stroked his jaw. "I think you might have to sit down. There's a lot to tell, and it will take some time."

Colin started at the beginning and told Shawn all that he had been told. "Well, I think I've shared everything that I was told."

Shawn rubbed his left forefinger over his bottom lip. "Do you remember the Leprechaun's name on the card?"

Colin sat back and folded his arms. "Let me see. I think it began with the letter "T", but I can't remember it."

Apparently, Katie O'Hara was standing outside the door listening to the whole conversation. She burst into the room. "Was the name Teague?"

Colin jumped up. Y-yes, that was it." He gave her a quizzical gaze. "How do you know his name?"

"Before I left Ireland, I was told about a Leprechaun named Teague and his friend Charlie." She turned to her uncle. "Uncle Shawn, I think that we have to talk to Father Flanagan, and the only way to be sure to see him is to attend the later Mass next Sunday."

Shawn nodded. "Yes, as long as he doesn't have an appointment after church that will be our best time. Let's pray that he doesn't have a prior engagement."

Katie waved her arms. "This is so wonderful. I had no idea the priest had knowledge of Leprechauns. His Bible stories are always interesting, but he's quite a priest." She tapped her lips with her right forefinger. "Believe me, he's nothing like the priests that I knew in Ireland or the priest at St. Marks here in Kade County."

Shawn folded his arms. "It was Mrs. Thomas who first told us about Father Flanagan and his Bible stories." He gestured with his left hand. "It's ten minutes closer for us to go to St. James, so we thought we'd give it a try."

Katie laughed. "We haven't been back to St. Marks since." She used her fingers to put her hair behind her ears. "Because Father Flanagan believes the Bible stories he tells, they become so exciting. It's like the people are alive; I just can't explain it. All I know is that I look forward to church."

Shawn ran his fingers through his black hair. "We have a busy week, and I'm sure Father Flanagan does. There's no way to see him before Sunday. Even then, will he have the time to hear this story?"

Colin raised his right hand and stroked his jaw. "Well, he is kind of really involved with this story. I'm sure he'll be glad to hear what you have to say about Teague the Leprechaun." He gave a slow grin. "To be honest, I'm truly eager to hear it myself."

Shawn shook his head. "We have to check some facts before we say anything."

Katie tapped her lips with her right forefinger. "What we need is for Father Flanagan to hear the story and then take us to the McGee's. It's imperative that Charlie hears the story, and Father Flanagan can help in the Bible part to understand."

Colin grabbed his shoemaker apron. "Should I inform Charlie and Mrs. McGee that you might be coming over with Father Flanagan? I will be there Sunday for lunch." He laughed. "If I know Mrs. McGee, she'll make lunch for everyone."

Katie gazed at Colin. "But what if we can't talk to Father Flanagan?"

Colin put his apron on. "I believe that Charlie and Mrs. McGee will still want to hear about the Leprechaun." He gave a slow grin. "Like I said, I'm quite eager to hear the story myself."

Shawn rubbed his left forefinger across his bottom lip. "Well, my lad, I feel that we really have to talk to Father Flanagan first. He may know more than we realize."

Katie jumped in. "Besides, like my uncle said, we want to make sure we know all the particulars before we go saying something that may not be true to the McGee's."

7

The End of the Rainbow

Shawn and Katie O'Hara went to the nine o'clock Mass, waited until Father Flanagan greeted the last person and Shawn walked over to him. "Father Flanagan, may Katie and I speak with you? It's quite important."

"Of course, Shawn." He bit the hangnail on his left thumb. "If you say it's important, I have the time." He pointed to his modest cottage. "Let's go in there and talk in private."

Shawn motioned for Katie to follow. She ran over and exhaled. "Thank you so much, Father for seeing us. We've been frazzled all week waiting for Sunday."

The priest blessed himself. "Oh my, you've really captivated my curiosity." He clasped his hands and shook them. "Now, I know why the Pringles cancelled their lunch appointment because of a family visiting from out of town. It was our blessed Savior's doing." He opened his door and beckoned them in. "Come in and have a seat. I'll just get us a pot of tea."

Shawn gestured with his hands. "Father, can we just wait for the tea? Besides, when we finish, I do believe that Mrs. McGee will have lunch waiting for us."

The priest fingered the rosary hanging from his waist with his right hand. "Does this have something to do with Charlie and his mysterious disease?"

Shawn nodded. "But it has more to do with Teague the Leprechaun." He pointed to his niece. "Katie knows the whole story, and it's quite a narrative."

❧

Colin's stomach was in jitters as he rode to Charlie's. "I'll tell you Riley, this has been a long week waiting for today." He rubbed his horse's neck. "I can hardly wait to hear the story about the Leprechaun and what it has to do with Charlie." He let out a heavy sigh. "I sure pray that when Mr. O'Hara tells Father Flanagan that he'll know what to do." He no sooner put Riley in the barn when Charlie and Toby were behind him. "You're a little earlier than usual, but that's good. Mum's making lunch, so we can talk awhile."

Colin raised his right hand and stroked his jaw. "I need to talk to you and your Mum about something very important."

Charlie's eyebrows scrunched up. "Is anything wrong?"

"No, I think everything is about to be right." He gestured with his right hand. "Let's get into the house before Father Flanagan, Mr. O'Hara, and Katie get here."

Charlie grabbed his head with both hands. "Why would Mr. O'Hara and his niece be coming here?"

"We need to get in the house, so I can tell you and your Mum what I know."

They both ran to the house with Toby in the lead. When they rushed in the back door, Maggie was leaning over the stove and they startled her. "Well, lads, it's not quite ready." She motioned to the wash bowl. "Why don't you two wash up and have a seat. I'll get you both a glass of milk while lunch is cooking."

Charlie gestured with his arms. "Mum, Colin has something real important to tell us. We don't need milk right now." He motioned to Colin. "Let's all sit. I don't think that I can wait any longer."

Maggie fingered her silver cross. "Colin, what is Charlie talking about?"

"Mr. O'Hara and his niece are visiting with Father Flanagan right now. Katie O'Hara knows the story about Teague the Leprechaun and his friend Charlie. She's probably telling the priest right now all about it."

Charlie slapped the sides of face with both hands. "They know about Teague." He gazed at Mrs. McGee. "Oh, Mum maybe they know how I turned green."

Maggie motioned for him to stay calm. "Let Colin finish his story."

Colin gave a slow grin and shrugged his shoulders. "It seems that's all I know about the story." He gestured with both hands. "The only other thing is that Father Flanagan, Mr. O'Hara, and Katie are heading here after they talk. I mentioned that you might have them for lunch."

Maggie stood up quickly. "I better get some more biscuits in the oven." She pointed to the stove. "I will have to get some more potatoes cooking. I'll just add another jar of green beans. The roast is enough to feed all of us and then some." She pointed to a pot on the hanging rack. "Charlie, would you get me that large pot in front of the small one?" She filled a bowl with potatoes from the bin. "If you boys would hurry and peel these for me while I get the biscuits going, we should be ready for company." She went to the back-storage room and brought out the biscuits that she had ready. "Thank God, I felt that I was to make a double batch of biscuits, but I can only bake one batch at a time with the roast in the oven."

The lads peeled the potatoes while Maggie tended to the meal. Once everything was about ready, she put a clean tablecloth on the table. The lads both took one of the Governor Carver side chairs from each side of the pine dresser with scrolled design, and then placed the chairs next to the side chairs already on each side of the table. Maggie took the special dinnerware displayed on the dresser and set a proper table for her guests. She had no sooner set the table when they heard the horses ride up.

Colin ran out to meet them. "Mrs. McGee is waiting for you. She has lunch ready." He opened the front door and led them to the kitchen.

Maggie and Charlie were standing on the other side of the table. Toby ran to greet the priest, jumped up on him, and began licking his face. Father Flanagan gave the dog a hug with both hands. "Well, I do believe he's happy to see me."

Colin pointed to Maggie and Charlie. "This is Mrs. McGee and Charlie." Then he motioned to Shawn and Katie. "This is Mr. O'Hara and his niece, Katie."

Maggie motioned for them all to take seats. "Please take a seat. Colin you can sit in your usual seat, Father Flanagan you take the chair next to Colin, Mr. O'Hara you can take that one, and Katie this is for you."

Shawn combed his hair away from his face with his fingers. "Mrs. McGee, would you please call me Shawn?" He gestured to the lads. "I am Mr. O'Hara to them, but I feel uncomfortable with you calling Mr. O'Hara."

Maggie reached out her hand. "It's agreed, if you will call me Maggie."

Shawn grinned and shook her hand. "That will be fine Maggie."

Father Flanagan clasped his hands and shook them. "We really must get on with this." He gestured at the food. "Suddenly, I seem to be quite hungry." He paused. "If you don't mind, may I give thanks?"

Maggie smiled. "I was just about to ask you to give thanks."

The priest bowed his head. "Lord, we thank you for this wonderful meal. We ask you to bless it, bless the hands that prepared it, and bless each one of us that partake of it."

"Amen!" They all said in unison.

Everyone filled their plates and Maggie poured the tea. As they began to eat, Father Flanagan started the conversation. "It seems that Katie knows the story about Teague and his friend. I know that you are all eager to hear it, but I feel that we need to wait until we've eaten and sit in your parlor." He fingered his rosary with his right hand. "This is quite a story, and I think we need to be in a more relaxed environment." He chuckled. "Besides, I really think that we need to eat."

After everyone helped to clean up, they all made their way into the parlor. "I believe that Shawn and Katie can sit on the sofa. Father Flanagan and I will sit on one of the chairs." She pointed toward the fireplace. "Charlie and Colin, you two will have to sit on the peg-leg stools on either side of the fire place."

Katie gestured towards the two butterfly trestle tables on either side of the sofa that held an Argand oil lamp with brass and china and a tall glass chimney. "Mrs. McGee, those lamps are exactly like the ones my grandmother in Ireland had." She paused. "I believe that the tables are the same also." She put her hair behind her ears with her fingers. "It was like I stepped back in time." She gazed at everyone. "Sorry, but it was such a strange feeling. I'll just take my seat."

All eyes were on petite Katie, who had to hold her waist-length black hair up to sit down. Her wide hazel eyes sparkled as she watched them all gazing at her. "I think before we start." She paused and gazed at Charlie. "May I please see the card with the peculiar message?"

Charlie jumped up with Toby at his heels as he ran to his room. When he returned, he handed the envelope to Katie. She opened the envelope, pulled out the card, read it, and handed it to her Uncle.

Shawn O'Hara gave a quizzical gaze as he read the card aloud.

"Charlie, did ye think ye got away?
Why did Teague ye disobey?
Did ye forget the power of old?
Say not, ye were not told.
Ye alone chose this fate,
When friendship ye did abdicate.
As brother to brother we were,
Till toward evil, ye did stir.
Ye took a charm to the green,

And hid in the night unseen,

Ye stole what was mine,

Now green, ye shall shine."

Katie nodded her head. "That's Teague for sure. The rascal really has a mess on his hands."

Shawn's eyes crinkled mirthfully. "He has no alternative, he must make it right. This is going to prove to be quite interesting as to what he's going to do."

Maggie fingered her silver cross. "Excuse me, but what is going on?"

Shawn rubbed his left forefinger across his bottom lip. "I'm sorry, Maggie. I forgot that you don't know the story and have no idea what we are talking about." He motioned to Katie. "Please tell them the story."

Charlie gestured with both hands. "Yes, after all, I am the one who is green."

Katie blushed. "Sorry." She straightened up in her seat. "What I have to tell is a remarkable story. You see, I spent the first ten years in County Kildare, Ireland, with my maternal grandmother. She told me about Teague. You see he is a Leprechaun who avoids contact not only with mortals and fairies, but other Leprechauns."

Charlie interrupted. "Why would he avoid contact with fairies and Leprechauns?"

Katie used her fingers to put her hair behind her ears. "It seems that Teague was quite a trickster and the fairies tried to drown him. My grandmother said they had forgiven him after he changed, but he still stays to himself. Perhaps, he is still ashamed of what he did."

Colin raised his right hand and stroked his jaw. "But if he avoids humans, who is this Charlie?"

Maggie motioned with her hands. "Will you lads let her tell her story? I'm sure all will be made clear when she is finished." She gestured with her left hand. "Please continue."

"You see, Teague had fallen out with a fairy tribe for all his tomfoolery. They waited until he settled down for the night and sprinkled fairy dust on him, which put him in a deep sleep. While he was asleep, they tied him with fairy rope, carried him to the Irish Sea, and dropped him in. Teague would have drowned if Charlie hadn't been walking along the shore and heard Teague's cry for help. He swam out to him and saved his life."

Charlie grabbed his head with both hands. "Wow! But why didn't he use his power of old to save himself?"

"Because Teague had no power over the magic twine of the fairies, he couldn't untie himself." She paused. "Anyway, as time went by, the two were like brothers. It was a unique relationship between a mortal and a Leprechaun, until Charlie became jealous of Teague's power. He became so deceived that he believed that if he had Teague's bright green amulet that he would have the same power." She held up the card. "As it reads, Charlie waited until Teague went to sleep and came in stealth at night. He stole the amulet, hid it in his satchel, and hurried away. Of course, when he went to take the amulet out of his satchel, it was gone."

Colin leaned forward. "Who stole it from Charlie?"

Katie motioned with her hand. "You see, a Leprechaun's magic amulet cannot be stolen. When a person lusts after it, he forgets that. He only thinks that he can steal it."

Charlie folded his arms and sat back against the wall. "What does the card mean that he was told about the power of old?"

"It's been passed down for generation upon generation in Ireland that the Leprechaun must declare a curse upon anyone who steals his amulet. If he doesn't, he loses all his power. The curse causes the person to be transformed into its green brightness. Charlie knew that. He also knew that it couldn't be stolen, except by one who is deceived."

Charlie grabbed his head with both hands. "Wait a minute! I thought the amulet couldn't be stolen."

Shawn rubbed his left forefinger across his bottom lip. "It can't be in a physical sense. You see, Charlie stole it in his heart. That's where the real crime took place."

"But how does that help me? How do I get rid of this green? I'm not that Charlie. Doesn't Teague know that he cursed the wrong Charlie?"

Shawn nodded. "Of course, he does. But he can't curse again for the same crime. It has to be that curse, on that card."

Charlie's eyebrows scrunched up. "I think this green is affecting my brain. I don't understand. If he knows that I'm the wrong Charlie, why doesn't he use his magic, take this card, and give it to the other Charlie?"

Katie leaned forward. "You have to understand the way of Teague. It's against his code of honor to steal from the innocent. He would have to steal the card to send it to the right Charlie."

Maggie threw up her arms. "Wait a minute! I think I understand. If Charlie gives the Leprechaun that card, the green is gone?"

Shawn combed his fingers through his black hair. "Yes and no. The green stays until the right Charlie gets the card and turns green."

Charlie's shoulders slumped. "Do you mean in order for me to be normal again, someone else has to have this curse?"

Father Flanagan bit the hangnail on his left thumb. "It's the Charlie who sinned against his friend." He gestured toward Katie. "According to Katie, he has had more than sufficient time to redeem himself. Teague gave him the complete seven years to come and stand before him and admit his crime." He gazed at Charlie. "The number seven means perfection. If Charlie had repented and confessed, then their relationship would have been perfectly mended."

Charlie gave the priest a quizzical gaze. "Okay, if Teague has to make this right, why did my glow go away when we did what the Bible said?"

Father Flanagan clasped his hands and shook them. "The book of Hebrews chapter eleven talks about faith. God will always honor faith, and he honored our faith by taking away the glow. But God couldn't do what Teague must do. You see, Teague made a grave error in not making sure the card was delivered to the right Charlie. When a person does wrong, it is up to that person to correct the wrong. God will not make right what is our responsibility to make right."

"Okay, that sounds fair. If I do a wrong, then it is my duty to make it right." He scratched the back of head with his right hand. "I also understand that it's not right for someone to be punished for the wrongs of someone else." He leaned forward. "But how do I give this card to Teague?"

Katie stood up and pointed out the window. "When we were riding up, I saw an old oak tree with huge roots above the ground with wild flowers growing all around it. You have to wait until dark and place the card near the roots."

Shawn nodded. "I believe that Teague has been watching you since he knew the card didn't get delivered to the right Charlie. He's probably more eager to have you normal than you are." He chuckled. "I wouldn't be surprised if he's in this room listening to us." He gestured with his left hand. "After all, Leprechauns can become invisible." He sat back and folded his arms. "You see, the longer that you are wrongly punished, the debt that he has to pay for his transgression gets greater and greater."

Charlie grabbed his head with both hands. "Wow! You mean that Teague could be invisible in this room? This gets more confusing all the time." He pointed up with his right forefinger. "However, I do understand that the Charlie who became a false friend should pay for his sin and not me." He gestured toward Colin. "If I did such wrong to him, I would deserve my punishment."

Father Flanagan clasped his hands and shook them. "Charlie, my lad you are amazing."

Maggie fingered her silver cross. "Well, I guess you all should stay for supper and we'll get that card at the roots of that old tree."

Shawn rubbed his left forefinger across his bottom lip. "Maggie, may I ask you about that cross?"

Maggie looked down at the cross. "What do you mean?"

"It's just that it's a plain silver cross and not a crucifix like other crosses."

Maggie took the cross between her fingers and held it up. "When my husband and I heard Father Flanagan teach that Jesus rose from the dead, Rory told me that Jesus is not dead any more. I looked at him a little confused. He then asked me why we have crosses with a dead savior on them." She gave out a heavy sigh. "After that, he bought me this silver cross to remind me that Jesus is alive. If Jesus is alive, then at the resurrection from the dead, all who believe in Jesus will be alive." She looked at the cross. "This cross reminds me that all who believe in Jesus and His resurrection will be raised from the dead someday."

Father Flanagan blessed himself. "Why didn't I see that before? I preach about the empty tomb, but the empty cross never occurred to me." He clasped his hands and shook them. "What a revelation."

Maggie got up. "If you all will excuse me, I really have to start preparation for supper."

Katie raised her right hand. "May I help?"

"Certainly. I won't refuse help." She turned to Charlie. "You have some catching up with feeding the animals, milking the cows, and all."

Colin gave a slow grin. "Charlie, I can help you? My Mum isn't expecting me home until late. I told her all that was going on. Besides, I did the chores for my sisters last night and early this morning. I didn't want to miss this."

Shawn combed his fingers through his black hair. "I have always wanted to milk a cow." He screwed up his face. "Do you think you can show me how to do it?"

Toby jumped and barked.

Charlie threw up his arms. "I'll be happy to show you how. This is like Christmas with me getting help."

Father Flanagan laughed. "Well, I think that perhaps I can be of more help in the kitchen."

As they all sat for supper, Father Flanagan gave thanks. When he finished, he addressed the others. "What do you think of Dr. and Mrs. Dixon leaving our church to go to West County? Since they are Charlie's godparents, they must have told you why?"

Maggie fingered her cross with her left hand. "Truth be told, we haven't seen them since the day after we went to Jordon Lake and Charlie's glow was gone. We had no idea that they were leaving." She paused. "How did you find out?"

"I was having supper with the Murphy's Friday night and they told me their neighbors left St. James." He blessed himself. "Oh my, if you don't know about them leaving, you don't know the other news."

"Like I said, we haven't seen them since then. They've suddenly been busy and haven't been here for their Wednesday or Sunday supper." She gestured with her hands. "They would normally be here tonight with us."

Charlie nodded. "We thought they were trying to find a cure for me. When they left the last time, Dr. Dixon said that he was convinced that medical science had the answer. I just figured they wouldn't come until they had the cure." He threw up his hands. "But I told them that I believed that somehow you would be involved in my cure."

The priest bit the hangnail on his left thumb. "It seems they offered Mrs. Cane a handsome amount of money to adopt the Morgan orphan. According to Mrs. Murphy, Judge Martin finished all the legal papers so that he could be christened John Henry Dixon by Father Wilson this morning."

Charlie threw his arms up. "Wow! That does beat all. Now we know why they have cancelled their visits. It's obvious that they no longer desire to be godparents." He hung his head. "But to be honest, I'm glad they're not here."

Maggie fingered her cross. "Yes, I believe that they're going in a different direction than we are. This is better for all of us." She patted the priest's left hand. "Father Flanagan, we're glad that you're here. We should have seen a lot of things before, but it's never too late to change." She gave a chuckle. "Our favorite priest taught us that."

Father Flanagan clasped his hands and shook them. "Speaking of change. I do believe that I have some excellent news about Peter Smith. It seems that lad had to learn a hard lesson. He turned sixteen about a month ago and started to work in the mine with his Pa."

Colin rubbed the back of his neck with his right hand. "I was wondering why he wasn't pestering me about Charlie." He shook his head and blew out a sigh. "He won't have time for any more shenanigans. Maybe that will put a lot of people at rest."

Father Flanagan threw up both arms. "It's much better than that. You see some time ago, I offered him a job helping me. But he had to agree to allow me to teach him to read and write a few hours a day. He turned me down flat and claimed that his Pa didn't need to read and write in the mine. Anyway, he came to me last Sunday night and asked if the job was still available. He said that he never realized what his Pa went through to work in the mine." He gestured with his hands. "The other wonderful thing is that he suddenly had an eye opener to what his Mum goes through. He said that all his Mum and Pa do is work and work all the time. With that revelation, it seems he thinks that if he gets educated that he can get a better job. I agreed to pay him double what he gets in the mine, which still isn't a whole lot. But his Pa wouldn't agree to him not working in the mine for less money than he gets from the mine." He chuckled. "So, I offered double to make sure that his Pa would agree."

Maggie clasped her hands to her heart. "That does make my heart glad. I know the lad has been trouble, but I still felt rather sorry for him. He seemed to be such a lost soul out of touch with reality."

Colin stood up and pointed outside. "It's about dark."

Charlie ran into the parlor and retrieved the card. "Do I have to do this alone?" He gestured toward Toby. "Surely he can come with me? After all, I have no idea how long it will take for Teague to come."

Maggie went to the spare room and came out with a couple of blankets. "You better wrap yourself in one of these and have one for Toby. It might get chilly overnight." She gazed at everyone else. "Colin you're welcome to sleep in Charlie's room. Father Flanagan can have the spare bedroom and Shawn you can sleep on the sofa, it is quite comfortable." She paused. "On second thought, I think that you will be more comfortable on the bed in my sewing room that I lay my sewing out on. It will only take a few minutes to make it up for you." She turned toward Katie. "You're welcome to sleep in my room; my bed is big enough for the two of us."

Everyone gave a sigh of relief, but Shawn uttered their thoughts. "I was wondering how I was going to get home and be back here before sunup." He laughed. "Now, I know why widow Cunningham asked if my mother could visit her for a few days. She and my mother love to play checkers. They sit for hours drinking tea and playing the game."

Father Flanagan clasped his hands and shook them. "I was thinking that I don't have any appointments tomorrow either. Of course, before all this I thought maybe something was wrong. Now, I know that it's because the blessed Savior had it all in control."

Charlie hugged his Mum and they all wished him well. "Come on, Toby, we have an adventure like none other."

Charlie and Toby hurried to the old oak tree and Charlie placed the card at the biggest root. Then he spread the blanket in place for Toby, wrapped himself up in his, sat on part of Toby's, and waited for Teague. At the sound of the cock's crow, Charlie woke with a start and Toby gave a bark. "Toby, we fell asleep and never saw Teague." Then he looked at the root and there was the card. "It looks like he never came." He picked up the card and his eyebrows scrunched up as he read it.

> *"Charlie, me lad, I do confess,*
>   *Of this, I've made quite a mess.*
> *Be sure I'll make things right,*
>   *Long before ye wake this night.*
> *Say not that Teague's unfair,*
>   *Upon my oath, I hereby swear.*
> *What I do, there is no hitch,*
>   *For Charlie, me lad, ye are rich.*
> *The rainbow, ye see, is yer clue,*
>   *Follow it till the end of the blue.*
> *Charlie, ye must do as yer told,*
>   *And ye shall find the pot o' gold."*

Toby rubbed his nose against Charlie's face. "Well, he did come. I don't know how we missed him."

Charlie went to get up when he heard Father Flanagan, his Mum, Colin, Mr. O'Hara, and Katie all scream, "Charlie! You're not green."

Charlie looked at his hands and slapped his face with both hands. "It's gone. I'm really not green." He stood up and his Mum went to give him a hug, but he motioned with his hands. "I must follow that rainbow before it disappears. Teague said that I must obey; I don't want to turn green again or something worse." Charlie ran as fast as he could with Toby at his side following the blue to the end.

Maggie and all the others threw up their hands in confusion and followed behind. At the end of the blue, Charlie stared and rubbed his eyes. "It's here! The pot of gold is here. Teague said it would be at the end of the blue." As he went to reach for it, there was a dazzle of light and there stood a three-foot-high Leprechaun with his red jacket, red breeches buckled at the knee, black stockings, and a hat that resembled a Puritan hat. Charlie fell backward. "T-Teague? You're here?"

> "Yes, me lad Charlie,
>> It is Teague ye see,
>> These months I've watched ye,
>> A friend ye are faithfully."

As the others arrived, they all stopped short. It was Father Flanagan that clasped his hands and shook them and voiced their surprise. "He's visible! It's Teague and he's visible."

Katie threw up her arms. "I never dreamed that I would ever see a Leprechaun in the flesh."

Maggie fingered her silver cross and stared at the little man. "Teague, I want to thank you for blessing my lad. From what I've heard, you truly are a changed Leprechaun."

Shawn rubbed his left forefinger across his bottom lip. "I never thought that I would ever meet a Leprechaun. This is truly amazing." He gestured with his left hand. "I have a real live Leprechaun standing in front of me."

Charlie scratched the back of his head with his right hand. When Father Flanagan gave me a birthday blessing and asked the blessed Savior to make it the best, I thought it turned out to be a curse." He motioned to Father Flanagan. "But after I read the story about Joseph in the Bible, I was convinced that God meant all this for good." He gestured with his right hand toward the gold. "It's a real pot of gold. Teague said it's mine. He gave it to me." Charlie let out a heavy sigh. "When I knew that God meant all this for good, I never thought that I'd be rich."

> *"Charlie, look at yer feet,*
> *Fer this is me treat.*
> *Others ye shall bless,*
> *Fer helping through the mess."*

Charlie looked down and grabbed his head with both hands. "There are three small pots of gold." He turned to look at those behind him and threw up his hands. "This is unbelievable." He gazed at Teague. "I'm to give one of these pots to Father Flanagan, Mr. O'Hara, and Colin. Right?"

> *"Charlie, me lad, ye got it right,*
> *This will surely help their plight,*
> *All have been selfless,*
> *Their help to others tireless."*

Charlie threw up his hands. "But I didn't think that Leprechauns ever gave away their gold. Why would you give us so much of your gold?"

Shawn gestured with his hands. "They don't unless they must redeem a terrible deed." He gestured toward Teague with his left hand. "To Teague, when you received the card, he committed such a deed. The cost of redemption is priceless. As far as a Leprechaun is concerned, his gold is a treasure that can't be valued."

"Tis the truth Shawn,
    Ye are not wrong.
But if truth be told,
    I'm pleased to give ye gold.
All are friends truly,
    Me gold I give ye freely."

Teague pointed to Father Flanagan.

"Now ye have what ye dreamed,
    To help those who are in need.
Our blessed Maker is pleased,
    That in ye is found no greed.
With helping others has been yer heart,
    And Teague will tell ye where to start.
Yer first one to help is Peter Smith,
    Apprentice him to the Kade County Coppersmith."

Toby stood up and walked over to Teague and licked his face.

Charlie folded his arms and laughed. "I believe Toby has accepted Teague as our friend."

Katie used her fingers to put her hair behind her ears. "I sure wish my grandmother could have met Teague." She gave a sigh. "But she smiled before she died and said Jesus had come to get her."

Father Flanagan blessed himself. "You can't meet anyone better than our blessed Savior." He clasped his hands and shook them. "What a glorious day that must have been for your grandmother."

While everyone was looking at Father Flanagan, they didn't notice that where Teague had stood was a card. When Charlie turned back to Teague, he saw the card. "Teague is gone!" He grabbed his head with both hands. "While we were all busy talking, he left without our thanking him." He threw up his arms. "How can we thank him?" He walked over and picked up the card.

"Charlie me faithful lad,
    Fer ye I'm truly glad.

Give ye friends their pot,
  And ye remember this spot.
As the days go by and by,
  On ye, I'll keep me eye.
When the time comes fer visiting,
  Here ye shall find Teague a sitting."

Charlie threw his arms up in the air. "He's going to visit me again." He ran over to Father Flanagan and gave him a big hug. "God truly did give me the best birthday blessing ever." Charlie went back to his spot and bent down to pick up a pot of gold. "Father Flanagan, this one is for you." He bent down and picked up another one. "Mr. O'Hara, this one is for you." He pointed to the third pot. "Colin, that one's for you."

Maggie walked over to her son and gave him a hug. "Well, Charlie I do believe that your sixteenth birthday brought a severe trial, but God did truly use it for good."

Charlie slapped his face with both hands. "But Mum do you realize that we can now fulfill Pa's dream for the farm? Pa always said that if we had some money to invest in the farm, that we could hire people to work it and make it a profitable endeavor." He pointed toward the barn. "You see that area behind the barn, I'm going to have a lodge built so that we can hire as many as we need to work the farm." He threw his arms up in the air. "We can enlarge our livestock, make bigger chicken coops for more chickens and eggs, and increase the number of crops that we grow." He grabbed his head with his two hands. "Oh my! I just remembered that Mr. Wilson is trying to sell his two-hundred acres and it's connected to our northern and western borders. Pa would definitely have bought it to increase our ability to be profitable."

Maggie fingered her silver cross. "I believe that the Wilson home has been all remodeled and has the most modern conveniences. They even have a large conservatory for herbs and plants for winter food." She cupped her hands to her heart. "Our blessed Savior truly made all this possible through Teague. We have been abundantly blessed."

Charlie laughed. "Yes, Mum, I think that we'll move into that house and use our house for a lodge for the workers. We can always add a few more bedrooms as needed."

Shawn rubbed his left forefinger across his bottom lip. "You know, I was thinking that I'd like Matthew Jones, the shoemaker in West County, to take my customers. After being here on this farm and milking the cow, I'd really like to have a farm of my own or help work one. The only reason I've been a shoemaker is because of my Pa, but I always felt that there was something missing. It was like I wanted to be more outside than inside."

Charlie threw up his arms. "Mr. O'Hara, why don't you, your Mum, and Katie move into our house and you can take over running the farm. I'll teach you all I know, and then you can teach the workers. If truth be told, I always wanted to be a lawyer." He grabbed his head with both hands. "Pa always said that he wished I could go to school and choose what I wanted to be. He had felt that I had a mind to do something important. Now, I can choose to be the lawyer that I always wanted to be." He pointed to the spot behind the barn. "We'll still build a lodge for the workers that we hire."

Colin raised his right hand and stroked his jaw. "I think that I'd like to go to school to be a doctor." He gestured toward Shawn. "Mr. O'Hara, I've been really grateful to you and what you've done for me and my family. It's just that I always wanted to be a doctor." He rubbed the back of his neck with his right hand. "My Mum always wished that she had a farm and could raise chickens like her Uncle in North County did. We use our land for planting vegetables that my Mum cans for the winter. Now, I can buy her the McKenna Chicken Farm and fulfill her dream." He gave out a heavy sigh. "This is so wonderful." Colin threw up his hands. "I've always liked Pete's Pa. Plus, I noticed that his Mum keeps that little cottage quite nice with all those children. It only has two bedrooms. All the boys share one bedroom, and Pete's parents sleep in the other room where they divided it for his sister to sleep." He nodded his head. "I'm going to give them our house. After all it has four bedrooms, a nice parlor, a big kitchen, and a spare room that my Mum uses for storage. Plus, we have five acres to plant in. I do believe that will make a big difference for the Smith's." He clutched his hands to his chest. "I am overwhelmed with all that God has blessed us with."

Shawn gestured his left hand towards Colin. "Did you know that Dr. Meadows wants to retire and sell his practice in a couple of years and move back to South County where he's from?"

Colin nodded. "Yes, I did know." He rubbed the back of his neck with his right hand. "This is incredible. I can be a doctor and buy Dr. Meadows' practice. I'll talk to him first thing this afternoon." He paused. "I can't wait to tell my Mum. The McKenna's place has a very large house with six bedrooms, a conservatory, about fifty acres, a stable, and other buildings. Every time my Mum has gone to buy eggs, she's commented on that house. Now, it's going to be hers and my sisters can all have their own room. I'll share with my little brother for the time being. Perhaps, Dr. Meadows will allow me to buy his practice now and I'll live there and help him out until I graduate." Colin ran over and took Charlie's right hand and cupped it between his. "I know it has been tough on you but thank you for being a true friend. We always talked about what we would really like to be, but we never let our desires interfere with our responsibility. And now it's actually going to become a reality."

Charlie grabbed his head with both hands. "I read a verse in the book of Psalms that says *Delight thyself also in the Lord and He shall give thee the desires of thine heart.* That's what Father Flanagan has been teaching us and now it's a reality. I think I'm in shock. We get our heart's desire and so do our Mums." He turned toward Father Flanagan. "I can't thank you enough for living what the Bible teaches. It was your faith that God honored to take away my glow and help us to see that Dr. and Mrs. Dixon don't believe the Bible. Anyway, I'm glad that we know the truth. It was you teaching that all is vanity that I found out how much of a fault it was with me." He gestured toward Colin with his right hand. "I was so guilty of vanity that I didn't even let my best friend see me. Best friends should stick together through thick and thin. Colin didn't care what color I was, he was my friend."

Father Flanagan clasped his hands and shook them. "Thank you, Blessed Savior! It seems like we're all going to have our prayers fulfilled. The Bible says to ask and ye shall receive and that's what I did." He blessed himself. "I have been praying to be able to help in such a way that lives can be changed for the better. I am so excited about Peter Smith." He gazed at Charlie. "Let me tell you that about a month in that mine changed that boy. Do you realize that in less than a week, he can already write his name and has learned the whole alphabet? He even asked me to help how he talks. He realized that he must sound like Charlie and Colin if he's going to improve his life. As a matter of fact, he's going to teach his whole family how to read and write." He paused. "Now that he's going to be apprenticed, he'll have to learn how to read and write on Sunday after Mass." He clasped his hands together. "The Blessed Savior just impressed on my heart to hire Pete's Pa. Andrew Smith has worked in that mine since he was eight years old. I'll hire him for double what he's making in the mine. Instead of working six days and seventy-two hours a week, he'll work only five days a week from eight until five. His son Joshua is about fourteen, I can hire him to work the hours that Pete was working and teach them both how to read and write." His eyes filled with tears. "I do believe that I am overwhelmed with our Blessed Savior's goodness."

Katie used her fingers to put her hair behind her ears. "Mrs. McGee, Colin told us that you make all the clothes that you and Charlie wear. I would sure like to know how to sew like that. I've always wanted to know how to make my own clothes, but both my grandmothers were too old to show me." She paused. "Do you think that you could show me?"

Maggie gave the lass a hug. "With you living so close to us, I'll be pleased to show you." She motioned with her hands. "I do believe that life is going to improve for all of us. With hiring enough workers to do the actual work, we'll be able to pursue our dreams."

Shawn combed his black hair back with his fingers. "Maggie, if you don't mind my asking? May I ask you what your dream is? We've all said what we want, but you've not said anything."

"My dream has always been to be able to spend more time just sewing. I truly love to sew; it seems to give me such pleasure. I'll admit that the other work can be a real chore at times, but sewing is my enjoyment. I could sew all day."

Father Flanagan bit the hangnail on his left thumb. "Charlie, you told the story about Joseph and how what was done to him was meant for evil, but God had meant it all for good. Well, the New Testament confirms that by a verse in the book of Romans chapter eight and verse twenty-eight that teaches if you love God that whatever He allows in your life will work out for your good. He doesn't say that the thing itself is good, but in the end it will all turn out to be for your good."

Charlie grabbed his head with both hands. "I understand! The glowing green was definitely not good and what was done to me was meant for evil, but God used it to make everything work out for my good and the good of others like it did for Joseph and his brothers."

Father Flanagan clasped his hands and shook them. "Amen!"